'Isn't it a lu

'That thinking y
am will protect
Just as it did a moment ago, when you kissed me.'

'It was you who kissed me,' Joanna flung back at him.

His eyes darkened. 'Then I must have been imagining the way you returned the kiss with interest, and the warmth there was when you put your arms around me, and when you held me just as close as I was holding you,' he murmured. 'Sure and it didn't seem that you had any objections to me kissing you.'

Elisabeth Scott was born in Scotland, but has lived in South Africa for many years. Happily married, with four children and grandchildren, she has always been interested in reading and writing about medical instances. Her middle daughter is a midwifery sister, and is Elisabeth's consultant on both medical authenticity and on how nurses feel and react. Her daughter wishes she met more doctors like the ones her mother writes about!

DANGER—DR HEARTBREAK

BY
ELISABETH SCOTT

MILLS & BOON®

All the characters in this book have no existence outside the imagination of the author, and have no relation whatsoever to anyone bearing the same name or names. They are not even distantly inspired by any individual known or unknown to the author, and all the incidents are pure invention.

First published in Great Britain 2000
Harlequin Mills & Boon Limited,
Eton House, 18-24 Paradise Road, Richmond, Surrey TW9 1SR

ISBN 0 263 82256 7

Set in Times Roman 10½ on 12 pt.
03-0008-52205

Printed and bound in Spain
by Litografia Rosés, S.A., Barcelona

CHAPTER ONE

JOANNA stood on the steps of the huge hospital, with the magnificent mountain behind it.

Table Mountain, and at last I'm here in Cape Town, ready to work at Groote Schuur Hospital.

She almost said the words aloud, to convince herself that this wasn't a dream. But, no, this was certainly no dream, it was very real. Around her, the bustle of a busy hospital surged—patients, relatives, doctors, nurses, porters, an ambulance drawing up, a stretcher being carried in.

It was the same as the hospital she had left behind in London, and yet very different. So many shades of colour in the faces around her, so many different languages she could hear. Hear, but not understand or even recognise, she realised with dismay.

For a moment, she wondered how she would fit in here, then she lifted her chin, in a gesture the friends she had left behind would have recognised, took a deep breath and walked in.

This is what I wanted, she reminded herself. A new start, in a new country. Not only wanted, but planned all those months ago.

Mrs Matama, the matron she was taken to, had her file open on the desk.

'We are very glad to have you here at last, Sister Boyd,' she said. 'Almost a year ago, I see, you intended being here. I am so sorry about your mother's illness and death.'

There was sympathy and kindness in the older woman's dark eyes, and Joanna's throat tightened.

'Thank you,' she said. 'We found out just after my application had been accepted, and...of course, I couldn't leave her.'

'Of course not,' Mrs Matama agreed. She stood up. 'We have a room for you in the nurses' home, although my sisters usually prefer to live out. But this will give you a chance to find your feet. If you have any problems, come to me.'

She lifted her telephone.

'Amelia, could you take Sister Boyd to her room? Thank you.'

Ten minutes later, Joanna stood in her new abode, her suitcase open on the narrow bed. A little different from the chaotic flat she had shared with three other nurses, round the corner from St Margaret's, she thought. And very different from the cottage in the small Surrey village, set in her mother's beloved garden, the garden she had insisted on working in as long as possible.

Joanna sat down on the only chair the room possessed, a wave of sadness and homesickness engulfing her. Perhaps it hadn't been a good idea, selling the house, asking the new owners if they would take over Shandy, the old Labrador, and Oliver, the cat. She had lived in that house all her life, first the three of them, herself and her parents, and then, after her father died, just the two of them. She could have let the house, could have kept it just in case she found she had made a mistake, in case she wanted to go back.

But, no, she had thought through all of that, and she had known that if she did that she wouldn't have come here so determined to make a go of it, so determined that this new start was the right thing for her.

She unpacked the few clothes she had brought with her, and they, with her uniforms, filled the small wardrobe. Before her trunk, which was coming by sea, arrived, she would certainly have to find somewhere else to live.

'Hi—have you settled in? I brought you a cup of tea. I'm Dorothy Marais, my room is along the corridor and I'm on maternity block, too. Sister Kenton asked me to look in on you.'

The girl in the doorway had dark, curly hair, blue eyes and a welcoming smile, and the mug of tea she was holding was steaming.

Joanna stood up, feeling better right away.

'Thanks so much,' she said. 'I was wondering how to go about things like tea.'

'There's a small kitchen at the end of the corridor,' the other girl told her. 'Sugar? No? We're allowed to boil water, and make toast, but that's all. The canteen is one floor down.' She wrinkled her nose. 'Don't expect too much from it, mind.'

'I won't,' Joanna assured her. 'I've known a lot of hospital canteens in my time. But I'll have to settle for it for the moment.'

And it wasn't too bad, she told herself later—plenty of salads, and the fish she chose wasn't too different from fish she knew. Dorothy wasn't there for supper, but the next morning she knocked on Joanna's door just after six. Joanna, already in her uniform, looked in some surprise at this towel-wrapped figure, its hair dripping.

'I'll be ready in ten minutes, if you don't mind waiting,' she said breathlessly. 'We can have breakfast, then I'll take you to our block. Meet you beside the kitchen.'

There was a mirror inside the wardrobe door, and Joanna had a last look at herself. She liked the short-sleeved uniform, right for a day when even this early she could see that the sun was shining. Doesn't feel like November, she thought, although already the steady downpour she had left at Heathrow seemed like a long time ago.

There hadn't been time to have her hair cut in these last few days, and it was just touching her shoulders. She was pretty sure hospital regulations would be the same here as in England, so she twisted her soft brown hair into a knot at the back. Yes, that looked better, more in keeping with a professional attitude from an English sister, and she wanted to start off on the right foot.

Impressively, Dorothy Marais was waiting for her, her hair only slightly damp, and Joanna was glad of her company in the crowded canteen, and grateful not to have to find her way through the long and bewildering hospital corridors, in and out of lifts, until the hungry cries of tiny babies told her she was in the right place.

'Sister Boyd? Thanks for looking after her, Nurse.'

The senior sister, Sister Kenton, comfortably built, her hair a soft grey, looked up from her desk in the duty room.

'Just let me finish these charts, and I'll be with you,' she murmured, more to herself than to Joanna. A few moments later, she looked up, smiling.

'That's it,' she said with relief. 'I'll take you round the block. You're on Labour Ward to start with—your file said you'd prefer that, and we need a sister there.'

There was a reassuring familiarity here, Joanna found herself thinking as she followed Sister Kenton along the corridor to the different wards. Women in early labour, walking around, doing their breathing exercises, anxious husbands, most of them pale and unshaven, nurses checking patients—oh, yes, she thought, it's good to be back at work.

And again, as she had noticed in the nurses' home,

there was an easy, casual air of friendliness. One or two of the older nurses looked really pleased to see her when Sister Kenton introduced her. But no wonder, Joanna thought, they certainly look as if an extra pair of hands could be useful.

'You'll have a chance to work in the nursery later, and in the ante-and postnatal clinics, and the breast clinic,' Sister Kenton told her. 'What will be new to you is our system of what we call MOUs, Midwives' Obstetric Units. These units are located in the townships, for the benefit of the people who live there. The mothers go in, have their babies and go home in a few hours. It's quite an experience, working out there. You need to have the confidence to make your own decisions because there isn't a doctor on hand.' She smiled. 'It's the closest we come to providing a National Health Service benefit.'

'And if there are any problems?' Joanna asked. 'A difficult delivery, or the baby needing specialised care?'

'Then Flying Squad goes to the rescue,' Sister Kenton told her. 'You'll certainly have to go out with them some time when you're on duty.'

They had now reached the end of the long corridor.

'This is the ICU—I might put you in there when we're short. I believe you have some experience.'

'Yes, I've worked a fair bit with prems,' Joanna said.

Sister Kenton's pager interrupted them imperiously.

'Back to Labour Ward,' she said briskly. 'And straight to work, Sister Boyd. They've had a quiet night, and now everyone has decided to deliver together.'

And if there's one way to make a nurse feel at home, Joanna found herself thinking a little later, this was it. Three deliveries in ten minutes. The first two she assisted, but with the third she did the delivery, and found herself holding her first South African baby, a plump, dusky little girl with a head of close dark curls.

'She will be called Inkulu,' the young mother said softly, as Joanna put her baby in her arms. 'That means firstborn in Xhosa.'

The young, fair-haired doctor, who had arrived just after Joanna had delivered the baby, said cheerfully, 'Just make sure you go to the clinic before you go home, so that Firstborn isn't followed by Secondborn too soon!'

'Oh, yes, Doctor,' the young mother said earnestly. 'This child must grow big and strong before another comes.'

'And I hope she sticks with that,' the doctor said a little later as he and Joanna accepted a quick cup of coffee in the duty room. He looked at her with such frank appraisal that Joanna couldn't take offence. 'I'm afraid there wasn't much time for formal introductions in the Labour Ward. I'm David Palmer.'

'I can see that you're Dr Palmer from your tag,' Joanna returned, unable to resist this. 'And I shouldn't have to tell you I'm Sister Boyd.'

He waited, eyebrows raised, and Joanna relented.

'Joanna Boyd,' she said.

'Welcome to Grotties, Joanna,' David Palmer said. 'Not very respectful, but I bet all hospitals get nicknames.'

'Yes, we all called St Margaret's Maggies,' Joanna told him. She put her cup down. 'I'd better get back, see what's happening.'

After that, the day flew by, with the pattern Joanna had so often found in labour wards—a lull, with a few women all in the first stage of labour and things looking well planned for their deliveries at staggered times, and then suddenly they were all in second stage and the midwives had to rush from one delivery to the next.

But she didn't mind. It was good to be back, doing the work she had been trained for, the work she loved. She had missed it in these last sad months when her mother had been so ill, but she'd had no regrets about resigning and caring for her mother. For so long her mother had been there for her, even after she'd grown up. Enjoying her stories of nursing life, giving loving sympathy over one or two broken romances and...just being there.

'You'll go to Cape Town...afterwards, Joanna?' she had said more than once in those last weeks. There had been no pretending between them. Her mother had wanted honesty from Joanna.

'Yes, I will,' Joanna had replied, as steadily as she'd been able to.

'Mind if we join you, Joanna?'

Glad to put her memories behind her, Joanna looked up to see Dorothy Marais and another nurse, plates of chicken and salad in their hands, beside her in the canteen.

Dorothy introduced the other nurse, Rose Hill, who was also in Maternity, but in the ICU.

'So you met our Dr Palmer,' Dorothy commented. 'What did you think of him?'

Cautiously, because you never knew in a hospital, Joanna said he seemed very pleasant.

Dorothy shrugged.

'He's all right,' she said dismissively. 'But very young.'

Amused, for David Palmer couldn't be any younger than Dorothy herself, Joanna found Rose Hill also trying to hide a smile.

'Dorothy likes older men,' Rose said.

'Just some older men,' Dorothy returned. 'And he isn't that old, anyway.'

'The perpetual Peter Pan, I'd say,' Rose Hill said drily.

'Just as well he's off on that course—things will be quieter around here.'

Intrigued, Joanna was on the point of asking who they were talking about but Dorothy turned to her.

'And what about you, Joanna?' she asked. 'Did you leave someone special in London?'

Joanna shook her head.

'No one special,' she said, with complete truth. Friends, yes, a good group of friends she would surely miss, but no one special.

Dorothy looked at her appraisingly.

'So did you come out here, hoping to meet someone?' she asked.

'Dorothy, you're being nosy,' Rose said.

The dark-haired girl shook her head.

'Not nosy, just interested,' she said disarmingly, and Joanna had to smile.

'No, I didn't,' she replied equably. 'I'm twenty-nine, and if I ever had any illusions about a prince on a white charger, coming into my life and sweeping me off my feet, well, I'm more realistic now. I don't think I'm the romantic kind. If and when I do meet someone, we'll probably just get along pretty well together, and that will be fine.'

Dorothy sighed.

'It's my Irish blood,' she said. 'My mother is Irish, and my father is Afrikaans, and I'm a pretty good mixture of them both. So I want my prince, but I'll settle for a white BMW instead of a charger!'

I like them both, Joanna thought later when the busy day was over and she changed out of her uniform in her small room. Dorothy, bright and bubbly, and Rose, quieter, older, but her brown eyes had been warm with sympathy when Joanna, replying to more questions from Dorothy, had told them about her mother.

It took only a few days for the ward routine to feel comfortable and familiar, and she found that language was no problem, for everyone she met, either nurses or patients, had enough English for communication to be possible.

She was doing her ward round one morning when the woman in the end bed called to her. Even before she said anything more, Joanna's eyes took in her extreme pallor and the beads of sweat on her forehead.

'I feel bad, Sister,' the woman murmured. 'And I think I'm bleeding.'

A swift examination confirmed that she was haemorrhaging, and Joanna, her voice steady, asked the student nurse to send for Dr Palmer. Sister Kenton, she knew, was at a staff meeting, and in any case Joanna herself knew what she had to do until the doctor came. She took pads from the locker, and applied pressure. Then, with the student nurse's help, she set up a drip.

'The doctor will be here soon,' she reassured the woman in the bed. 'That's right, lie still.'

She heard the swift stride of the doctor's feet coming towards her, but she dared not turn round, keeping the pressure steady.

'Good, Sister, you've got things well under control. Mrs Thorpe, I'm going to give you an injection.'

Not David Palmer. And not the older Indian doctor, Dr Rajbansi. Instead— It couldn't be. It couldn't possibly be. But it was.

Professional training took over, and Joanna's hands were steady as she assisted the doctor. The doctor. Tall, with thick, dark hair and dark blue eyes, his face lean and brown, browner than she remembered it. Very good-looking. Oh, yes.

Jake O'Connor.

He hadn't recognised her, but she wouldn't have expected him to.

'You did a good job, Sister...Boyd,' the doctor said, glancing at her name tag as they left the ward together. 'She's still in shock, but she'll be all right. We'll do a blood test later, but thanks to your quick action she hasn't lost too much. You're new, aren't you?'

'Yes, I am,' Joanna replied, and she didn't care if her voice sounded as curt as she thought it did. 'If you'll excuse me, Doctor...'

His eyes were an even darker blue in the deeper brown of his face.

'No cup of coffee before I go?' he asked her.

He knows just the effect that smile has, Joanna told herself. But not on me. No, sir.

'I'm sure one of the nurses will be only too glad to see to that for you,' she said coolly.

The dark blue eyes looked down at her thoughtfully.

'Sure and you're right, Sister,' he murmured. She had forgotten the charm of the Irish accent in that deep voice. Now there was laughter in his eyes. 'It's a bit much for me to be expecting a sister to make me a cup of coffee.'

Joanna, walking out of the duty room, her head high, was all too conscious that he was watching her.

'Isn't he terrific?' Dorothy Marais said breathlessly later, when she and Joanna met in the small kitchen of the nurses' home. 'An absolute honey—those eyes, and that smile!'

'Terrific? Who?' Joanna asked, knowing very well who Dorothy meant.

Dorothy's eyes widened.

'Jake O'Connor, of course,' she said.

Joanna shrugged.

'He's good-looking, sure, but I can't stand these doctors who think they're the answer to a maiden's prayer. Every maiden.' And then, because she would look foolish if it came out later, she added casually, 'He was the same at St Margaret's, where I trained and worked.'

Dorothy carefully put down the cup she was holding.

'You mean you know him?' she asked, awed. 'You know Jake O'Connor?'

Joanna shook her head.

'Not really,' she said. 'I know him, but I doubt if he would remember me.'

And that, she thought, was just as well. Because she was pretty sure that Dr Jake O'Connor wouldn't be particularly pleased to see anyone who had known him at St Margaret's.

'Did you know he was here?' Dorothy asked, obviously fascinated.

Joanna shook her head.

'No,' she said, 'I didn't.'

And I refuse to let it bother me, she told herself firmly back in her room. He's a doctor I have to work with, that's all. The fact that I know he's an absolute—an absolute—Bastard? Bounder? Cad? Even in her thoughts, words failed her.

She hadn't known Helen Johnson very well, only that she'd been in Theatre, and engaged to the rather devastating Dr O'Connor. Jake O'Connor, who'd just had to smile and any nurse in St Margaret's would have fallen at his feet. Which they had, regularly, before he and Helen had got engaged. Two of the Beautiful People, Joanna had sometimes thought, Jake O'Connor so tall and dark, and with these incredible dark blue eyes, and Helen, tall also, slim and blonde.

But there had been nothing glamorous or beautiful about Helen Johnson that day in the small rose garden behind the hospital when Joanna, having a fresh-air break before going back to the ward, had found her there. Her blonde hair had been dishevelled, her eyes red, and she'd been so distressed that Joanna couldn't have pretended there'd been nothing wrong.

'Helen, what is it?' she asked.

The other girl held out her left hand, with a white band where the sapphire engagement ring everyone had admired, had been.

'Jake doesn't want to marry me,' she said shakily. 'He's broken our engagement.'

'Broken your engagement?' Joanna repeated, taken aback. 'But...why, Helen? You always looked so happy, so—so good together.'

Helen shrugged.

'I thought so, too,' she said shakily. 'But I should have known Jake just wasn't the faithful kind. I should never have trusted him.' Tears filled her eyes again. 'He's just that kind of man.'

I know that kind of man, Joanna thought, and a bitterness she had tried so hard to forget swept through her whole body. Cliff Denton had been like that—the promises he had made, the assurances that she'd been the only girl for him—and all the time there had been the girl he'd been seeing in Edinburgh every time his consultant's job had taken him there, and the one in Bristol. And probably others. She had been the last to know, because she'd trusted him. Oh, yes, Joanna thought, I know that kind of man too well.

She made comforting sounds, as well as she could, and

Helen scrubbed her red eyes, tidied her hair and went back to Theatre.

She left soon after that, and there was talk that she was close to a breakdown. Then Jake O'Connor left, and pretty soon the hospital had other things to think about and to talk about.

But Joanna knew she wouldn't easily forget what sort of man Dr Jake O'Connor was, and the way he had treated the girl he was engaged to. Sure, engagements could be broken, and people could change their minds, but you'd have thought he'd been around enough to have known his own mind when he'd asked Helen to marry him. Known it, and been able to stick to it. Obviously, like Cliff, he just wasn't the faithful kind.

Anyway, Joanna reminded herself now, that was a long time ago, and in another country, and she certainly wasn't going to tell Dorothy or anyone else what she knew about the good-looking Irish doctor.

But she herself wasn't about to be bowled over by his charm, like most of the other nurses. And sisters, even Sister Kenton, clearly had a soft spot for him. Everyone but me, Joanna told herself with some satisfaction. And a good deal of her satisfaction came from knowing that Jake O'Connor was very conscious of that. Sometimes she found him looking at her thoughtfully as she replied coolly to his questions about a patient or stood by to assist him with a difficult birth. She refused to be drawn into any exchange that wasn't to do with their work.

Work that she enjoyed, and found fulfilling, as she always had. Labour Ward was busy and bright, and the pain her patients went through was always forgotten in the joy of their newly born babies.

Dorothy Marais and Rose Hill told her they were hoping to move out of the nurses' home as soon as they found somewhere to rent, and they asked her if she would be interested in joining them.

'I'd love that,' Joanna replied, delighted, for there was nothing home-like about her small and spartan room, and soon her trunk would arrive, with more clothes and with the few possessions she hadn't been able to bring herself to part with. The thought of sharing a proper home appealed very much to her, and when Rose found an old house in Observatory, just down the road from the hospital, the three of them went to see it.

'It's bigger than we actually need,' Rose pointed out, when they had admired the high-ceilinged rooms, the spacious kitchen, which had been nicely modernised, and the roomy bathroom, with both a bath and a shower. Joanna, admiring the wide and shady veranda, was informed that in South Africa this was called a stoep. 'We can each have our own room, and there's still the smallest bedroom.'

Dorothy walked over to the window, and inspected the wooden shutters.

'We could ask David if he'd like to join us,' she said, so casually that Joanna and Rose couldn't help their eyes meeting in shared amusement for a moment. 'I happen to know he's looking for somewhere, and it isn't a bad idea to have a man around the place.'

'Not a bad idea at all,' Rose agreed gravely, 'but I thought you couldn't be bothered with him because he's so young.'

'He is very young,' Dorothy returned, her cheeks pink, 'but I don't mind having him around, sort of like a—like a brother for all of us.'

The 'brother', it turned out, was only too pleased to be given the chance, and before the end of the month the four of them were installed in the house. Joanna, encouraged by the advantageous rate of exchange, bought a small second-hand car, and it sat in the off-street parking beside David's shabby but faithful Beetle.

She didn't use her car to go to the hospital as it was only a short distance up the hill and she loved the early morning walk when the air was fresh, before the heat of the day reminded her that she was living in a hot country now.

More and more, as she worked with Jake O'Connor, she had to admit that she respected his skill and his knowledge. And, she would sometimes think ruefully, his speed, for very often there was little time to send for him.

Dealing with an undiagnosed breech delivery one afternoon, she could see that there wasn't time for any of the doctors to get there and that she would have to deliver this baby herself.

Swiftly, expertly, she did an episiotomy, reassuring her patient, anxious now, that this was necessary.

'It's to make the delivery easier, Mrs Pryce,' she said. 'There—that wasn't too bad, was it? Now, just do what I tell you. Push when I say, and stop when I say.'

Across the bed her eyes met the staff nurse's, and she knew that the younger girl realised the dangers of a breech delivery. There could be intracranial damage if the head came out too quickly, but the episiotomy she had done should help to prevent that.

'Right, a good push,' she told her patient. Gently, she eased the baby's tiny bottom out. 'Now, stop pushing. Wait...now you can push again.'

Absorbed, she eased the slippery little body out gently, carefully. There was always this moment of wonder, holding a newborn baby, she thought. And more and more each time a stirring of something deep inside her, something she didn't want to admit even to herself. It was only when she handed the baby boy to her staff nurse that she realised Jake O'Connor was there, watching.

'Well done, Sister,' he said, and above his mask his blue eyes were smiling. 'I was ready to step in, but I wasn't needed. Left sacro-anterior position, wasn't it? Not easy.'

In spite of all she knew and felt about this man, Joanna was very conscious of her flush of pleasure at his praise, which he didn't give lightly. She had gathered that in the time she'd been working with him.

Whatever else Jake O'Connor is, she admitted to herself, he is undoubtedly a good doctor. And that's why I'm pleased that he praised me.

'We should have a house-warming party,' Dorothy suggested, shortly after they'd moved into the house.

'We can't afford a party, with these new curtains and the chairs we had to get for the kitchen,' Rose pointed out.

Dorothy shrugged.

'We don't need money to have a party,' she said. 'People will bring things. Drinks and things. It will be a good chance for you to get to know people, Joanna.'

Amused by the guileless voice and the wide-eyed innocence in the younger girl's eyes, Joanna couldn't help smiling.

'Come on,' Rose said, 'you just like parties.'

'So did you last year, before Andrew went back to be a GP in Kimberley,' Dorothy returned. 'Couldn't he come, Rose?'

Rose shook her head.

'He's too busy,' she said firmly. 'And, anyway, you know we're saving hard. But, yes, a party might be a good idea. When is it going to be, do you think? Or hadn't you planned that far?'

As soon as possible, Dorothy told them, because in just over a week it would be December and, as she said darkly, Things Hot Up Then.

It would be nice, Joanna couldn't help thinking, to get to know people now that she was beginning to feel as if she was putting down some roots by moving into the house. And by people, she didn't necessarily mean men, she told herself. Not that she would mind meeting one or two nice fellows, though preferably not doctors—she had one or two less than fortunate memories of dating doctors. But someone to go around with a bit, to begin to get to know this beautiful city she was living in.

'Is Jake O'Connor coming to our party?' she asked Dorothy casually a few days later.

Dorothy looked up from the list she was making.

'If he can,' she said indistinctly, a pencil in her mouth. 'Depends whether he's on call or not. Why?' She took the pencil out of her mouth. 'Changed your mind about him?'

'Not at all,' Joanna replied with conviction. In fact, she thought, I'll be only too glad if he doesn't come.

And on the night of the party it looked as if she could be glad, for there was no sign of the big Irish doctor. Joanna, agreeing with a rather nice accountant that, yes, the weather here was certainly quite different from London in November and, no, she hadn't been to the Waterfront yet, looked around the crowded, noisy room and thought that it really had been a good idea of Dorothy's to have a party. Already, people from two houses down had invited them to their party, and the two old ladies across the road had insisted on making crunchies for them.

'No, dear, we won't come,' the older one had said, not realising that all Dorothy and Joanna had been doing had been warning them about the noise and apologising in advance. 'And don't you worry one bit. Maud and I were young once, too.'

'A long time ago, Sylvia,' her sister returned. 'And, anyway, we're both too deaf to be bothered by the noise. Just don't let anyone park in our driveway, that's all.'

Yes, a good idea, the party, Joanna thought when the accountant turned to greet someone he knew. And then, at the door, she saw Jake O'Connor. He was alone, but only for a moment. Two of the nurses from Surgical hurried across the crowded room to greet him, and five minutes later Joanna happened to see him dancing with one of them. Ten minutes after that he was standing talking to the red-haired sister from Casualty. Joanna knew her because a few days ago she had brought up to them a young woman on the point of having her baby.

He hasn't changed at all, Joanna thought, and she remembered having seen him with quite a few different girls before he and Helen had got engaged. He certainly spreads his favours around.

It looked as if it might be time to heat the sausage rolls someone had brought, and the delicious samosas. She couldn't see either Rose or Dorothy, so she went through to the kitchen, quite glad, for the moment, to be somewhere quieter and more peaceful.

'Sure and they didn't tell me your middle name was Cinderella.'

She swung round as Jake O'Connor came into the kitchen and sat down at the table, watching her while she put the trays into the oven.

'I see you've been managing to do a bit of sunbathing,'

he said conversationally, and Joanna was very conscious of the only just decent boob tube she was wearing.

'It matches your eyes,' the Irishman said, leaning forward earnestly. 'But I'm sure you would know that.'

Joanna felt her cheeks grow warm. Yes, she did know that, having chosen the sea-green colour of the top and the Indian cotton skirt very carefully.

'There's food next door,' she said brusquely. 'I'll bring these through when they're ready.'

He sighed.

'Do I look so hungry, then? No, it wasn't food I was looking for. I had said hello to my other two hostesses, and it seemed only right to look for you. My mother always taught me to do that at parties. And to say my thank-yous when I left.'

For a moment, Joanna had an absurd vision of a small, dark-haired boy at a party, doing exactly what his mother had told him to do. She had to fight to keep back a reluctant smile.

'And now that I've done the right thing, would you like to dance?'

'No, thank you,' Joanna replied. 'I'm busy right now.'

The dark blue eyes considered her thoughtfully.

'I've wondered, sometimes, Sister Boyd—Joanna—if you really are rather unfriendly, or if perhaps you're playing some game?'

Joanna looked up at him, not bothering to hide her anger.

'I'm not playing anything, Dr O'Connor,' she returned. 'I don't play games.'

She could only think, later, that it had been the disconcerting effect of that steady blue gaze that had made her say quickly—unwisely, 'And anyway, it's much too crowded to dance.'

Jake came towards her purposefully.

'Not in here,' he said softly, and the next moment his arms were around her, drawing her close to him. Short of actually struggling, there was nothing Joanna could do, except move with him in his arms.

For a moment his finger touched her lips lightly.

'Don't speak—just dance,' he murmured.

And then his arms were around her again, holding her close to him. Very close.

I don't know what came over me, Joanna thought later, mortified. Because she did just what he told her, moving with him, his body and his arms telling her what to do, to the faint strains of the nostalgic music from the other room.

And suddenly Joanna was in command of herself again. She drew back, on the point of telling him that she had come here from St Margaret's, that she had known Helen Johnson.

'Dr O'Connor,' she began, but at that moment, his bleeper sounded, startlingly loud even against the music.

'Damn,' he said forcibly. 'I'm on call—I have to go.'

Once again his finger brushed her lips.

'We'll do this again,' he said softly, and then he was gone, striding out of the room, his dark head purposeful.

Joanna took a deep breath.

Oh, no, we won't, she told him silently. And I really don't know what came over me. It's so long since I danced, that's all, and I was taken by surprise. That's all.

But that night, when the party was over, and the old house was silent, she lay in her room wide awake, unable to forget how she had felt, with Jake O'Connor's arms holding her so close to him, with his body warm against hers.

* * *

Having her little car made such a difference, Joanna found, as she began to make cautious little expeditions in her time off. It amused her when people told her seriously to try to get back before the rush hour, but she managed not to say they should see a real rush hour around London.

The accountant she had met at the party, Trevor, took her for dinner to a seafood restaurant at the Waterfront one night.

'I don't think I'll ever take this wonderful weather for granted,' Joanna said, when they had finished dinner, and were standing beside the small bridge over the harbour, with the brightly lit shops and restaurants around them. Table Mountain, floodlit for the summer season, rose majestically above the city.

Trevor smiled.

'Last Christmas my brother and his family were here—they live in Canada now. When we took the dog for a walk beside the river his little girls used to run ahead of us, shouting, "No shoes, no coats!" They couldn't believe it.'

'Neither can I,' Joanna agreed, for she was wearing a sleeveless cotton dress and her sandalled feet were bare. The warm night air on her bare arms and legs felt like silk.

It was late when Trevor took her back to the old house which she was already beginning to think of as home, and the only light on was the one beside the front door.

'Thank you, Trevor, it was a lovely evening,' Joanna said.

'We'll do it again—I'll ring you,' he said.

In the dim light of the stoep he kissed her, his lips gentle and warm. Joanna wondered what he would say if she were to tell him that it had been a long time since she'd been kissed goodnight after a date. It was a pleasant kiss, an enjoyable kiss, she thought as she went into the house and through the dark passage to her own room. But…no spark. Not that she was looking for sparks, she reminded herself hastily. A friendship like this would do very nicely.

She was beginning to get to know the people she worked with, and one of the young student nurses, Thandi Kepenza, had attached herself to Joanna.

'Sister Boyd,' the young girl said one day, tragically, 'I'm still waiting for a delivery, and next week I will be in the nursery, and it will be weeks before I'm back on Labour Ward!'

'I know, Nurse,' Joanna sympathised, 'and it was a shame that Mrs Nguli had to have a Caesarean when you had specialled her for all that time. But the foetal heartbeat had dropped below one-twenty, and the baby was at risk—you know that.'

The young nurse nodded.

'I know, Sister, and I'm glad the baby is fine, but I did feel cheated.'

The fierce honesty in her voice made it difficult for Joanna not to smile.

'I can understand that, Nurse,' she agreed. 'You do still have a few days and, I promise you, if it's at all possible you'll have your delivery.'

However, as the days passed she began to think that Thandi was going to be disappointed. For some reason, which she and other midwives had often commented on, the quick and easy births seemed to happen at night, and the longer, more difficult ones through the day.

'I agree, Sister,' Jake O'Connor said, coming into Labour Ward as Joanna was saying this to Thandi. 'And Mrs Grant, who has just come in, is here because her baby is in a breech position, so no luck there. But stick with

Sister Boyd, you'll learn a lot from her. Let's have a look at Mrs Grant, then.'

He smiled, and Joanna knew she wasn't imagining that the dark blue eyes lingered on her face, half teasing, half amused at her lack of response. She and her student nurse followed the tall, white-coated figure to the bed at the end of the ward.

'He's wonderful, isn't he?' Thandi said breathlessly. 'Everyone thinks so.'

Everyone but me, Joanna thought. But I'm the only one who knows what he's really like.

And not for the first time since the night of the party, she found herself wishing that her attempt to get things into the open with the big Irish doctor hadn't been prevented. Because it seemed more and more important to her that Jake O'Connor should know what she thought of him, should know why he needn't bother wasting his time, and his charm, on someone who had seen the heartbreak of the girl who had loved him.

Because I know so well what it's like, she thought, to love someone, to trust him and to be let down.

And that, she reminded herself, is something I'm not likely to forget.

CHAPTER TWO

JAKE O'CONNOR stopped, and turned to Joanna and her student nurse.

'Right, Sister,' he said briskly, 'before we have a look at Mrs Grant, let's hear how you go about passing on your experience to your student nurses.' His eyes were guileless, but Joanna was certain he was having trouble keeping his face as straight as it was.

Joanna was determined she would do no more than take this at face value, so she turned to the young girl.

'Nurse Kepenza, what are the possible dangers in a breech presentation?' she asked.

'Intracranial damage, hypoxia, venous congestion and cord compression,' Thandi replied promptly.

Joanna nodded.

'You certainly know your Maggie Myles,' she said, referring to the midwives' bible.

She looked up at the doctor. 'Anything else you would like me to go through, Dr O'Connor?' she asked. 'Normally, I would explain what I was doing as I examined the patient, but, of course, you will be doing the examination so no doubt you will be explaining as you go?'

There was no mistaking the amusement in his eyes, and Joanna felt her cheeks grow warm.

'Sure and you're right, Sister,' he replied smoothly.

Joanna couldn't help thinking, And one up to me, Dr O'Connor. You put me on the spot—now I've turned the tables. And now, she thought dispassionately, he's turning the charm on the patient.

'Mrs Grant, I was counting on seeing you round about now, you being one of my very special patients. Let's see what this baby of yours is doing.'

His hands were sure and strong as he examined the woman in the bed, and Joanna, watching with somewhat unwilling professional admiration, was conscious of a momentary pause before he turned to her.

'I'll do an internal now, Sister. Gloves, please.'

For a moment his eyes met hers, and Joanna saw that now there was nothing but a competent doctor, doing the job he did so well. And telling her something.

When he had finished he said, 'Has the baby been very active recently, Mrs Grant?'

Mrs Grant nodded.

'You bet it has, Doctor,' she replied feelingly. 'This is my third, and the other two didn't do this much kicking right at the end. Proper little soccer player in there, my husband says.'

Jake turned to Joanna.

'The baby has turned on its own, so...no breech presentation. And the head is well down so it should be a nice easy delivery.'

He smiled, and Joanna couldn't help returning his smile.

Young Thandi had already realised what this could mean. Her dark eyes widened.

'Mrs Grant, your little soccer player has decided to be a good team player, and we should have you in Labour Ward very soon. Sister?'

Joanna followed the doctor, leaving the young nurse rubbing her patient's back and talking cheerfully to her.

'You're going to ask if your student nurse can do the delivery, aren't you?' Jake asked her.

'It should be normal and straightforward, and she's

been waiting for a delivery. I'll stand by, of course,' Joanna said.

Jake nodded.

'That's fine with me. I rely on your judgement.' He looked at his watch. 'I'll be at a meeting, but you can send for me if you need me.'

He strode off down the corridor, his dark head high, white coat flying. Joanna watched him go, and was thrown into confusion when he turned at the lift and raised a hand in farewell.

He would be smiling, she was sure, because he'd caught her looking at him, she knew, annoyed at herself.

She waited until Thandi had made her patient comfortable, and then called her to the duty room.

'As long as nothing changes, this is your baby, Nurse,' she said.

The girl's face lit up.

'Oh, Sister, I was hoping when Dr O'Connor said the baby was no longer breech.'

Half an hour later Joanna saw that this was going to be a quick delivery, and she turned to Thandi, scrubbed and gloved beside her and trying, not too successfully, to hide her breathless eagerness.

'All yours, Nurse,' she said.

The head was showing, and the young nurse gently held it and eased it out. Then, with a sudden slippery movement, the shoulders followed, and the baby was born.

'You've got your little soccer player, Mrs Grant,' Thandi said triumphantly. 'And he's gorgeous!'

Not quite professionally distant, Joanna thought, hiding a smile, but she knew how it felt, delivering that first baby.

'It's the most marvellous thing,' Thandi said later in

the duty room. 'Holding that newly born baby and handing him to his mother—it was wonderful.'

'And I'll tell you something, Nurse,' Joanna said, taking the mug of coffee the young nurse handed her. 'It goes on being marvellous. You never do take it for granted. I felt just the same with the baby I delivered this morning as I did with my first delivery.'

'And that goes for me, too, Sister,' Jake O'Connor said from the doorway, and there was nothing but sincerity in his eyes. 'I just looked by to see how your delivery went, Nurse.'

'It was wonderful, Dr O'Connor,' Thandi said, breathless again. 'Thank you, both of you.' Suddenly embarrassed, she murmured something awkwardly and scurried out of the room.

Jake O'Connor looked at Joanna, his dark eyebrows raised.

'Would you like a cup of coffee, Dr O'Connor?' Joanna asked. After all, he had been especially kind about this delivery, and the doctors were usually given coffee.

She handed him a mug of coffee. For a moment, as he took it from her, his fingers touched hers. Joanna moved her hand quickly.

Jake O'Connor took a sip of his coffee, and looked at the blue mug.

'I'm just after wondering, Sister,' he said thoughtfully, 'whether this might be in the nature of an olive branch.'

'It's just a cup of coffee,' Joanna returned brusquely.

And, of course, it was, she told herself when he had gone. Just because she admired him as a doctor, that didn't mean that she had changed her mind in any way about him as a man.

A day or two later, Joanna was walking down from the hospital just after two—for this was one of her early days—when a car stopped beside her.

'I'll give you a lift,' Jake O'Connor said.

'It isn't far,' Joanna replied.

'I know that, but it's a hot day and it's just a bit undignified to be standing, arguing, here in the street, is it not?'

It was, Joanna realised from the amused glances of two theatre nurses walking past. Without another word she got into the car.

'Have you been to the Rhodes Memorial yet?' Jake asked, taking her by surprise so that she didn't see further than the question. She replied that, no, she hadn't been there yet.

'Then it's time you went there,' he said decisively, and at the next traffic lights he turned round and headed back up the hill and then away from the hospital. 'Don't worry, Joanna, this is all very innocent. The view is wonderful, and there's tea and scones, and so freshly made they just melt in your mouth.'

Joanna had recovered her composure, and she was determined to remain cool and in command.

'One thing I'd like to know. Why is it, Dr O'Connor,' she asked, 'that you have the nerve to assume that I have nothing better to do than to be taken sightseeing by you? Do you think your famous Irish charm lets you do just what you want?'

The dark-haired man looked down at her, amusement in his blue eyes. Before he replied he turned off the main highway and headed along a small wooded road up the side of the mountain.

'I admit I do have a nerve,' he said, 'assuming that you weren't hurrying off for a date perhaps. But I wouldn't have thought, myself, that there was anything either charming or famous about a fellow from Ballantony, and it no more than a small town south of Dublin, but it's nice to be told that.'

They had reached the top of the road, and he parked his car. Joanna managed to get out and shut her door, just as he reached her.

'I like a touch of independence, girl dear,' he murmured, but Joanna ignored that.

I'm going to tell him, she thought. I'm going to tell him now.

But he was striding ahead of her up an uneven set of steps.

'I see a tourist bus coming,' he said over his shoulder. 'Hurry, so that we can get a table with a good view.'

When Joanna reached the small wooden gate he was already claiming a table at the far side of the group of wooden tables with their bright tablecloths, each one shaded from the heat of the sun by a large umbrella.

'I still find it a treat, to be able to sit and eat outside, like this,' he said disarmingly. 'Tea for two, and scones with jam and cream. Or would you rather have carrot cake?'

Joanna shook her head. There were too many people around, she realised. There was no way anyone could have a private conversation.

'There is the hospital,' Jake said, pointing out the huge, sprawling buildings. 'And the sea, behind the city.'

Joanna leaned forward, looking at the grassy slopes below them.

'Look,' she said, excitement making her forget her reserve, 'what are these animals down there?'

Jake followed her pointing finger.

'Just a couple of wildebeest and a zebra or two,' he said casually. 'You'll know the wildebeest as a gnu. Do you know the Flanders and Swann song?' And in a very pleasant baritone that had the group at the next table looking round, startled, he sang softly, "I'm a g'nu, how do you do? I'm the—"

'Yes, I know it,' Joanna replied hastily, glad to see their tea and scones arriving.

The bus party, mostly German tourists, arrived then, taking up all the free tables, and there was even less chance for her to say what she wanted to say. And now that she had made up her mind that this was her chance, she didn't want to put off.

They left the tea-garden and walked back to the top of the path, with the stone memorial to the left.

'"Immense and brooding spirit",' Jake murmured, reading the inscription about Cecil John Rhodes on the wall. He let her finish reading it, and then, his hands on her shoulders, he turned her to face the other way. 'Now for the real view,' he said softly, and there was something in his voice that made her look at him curiously.

They were at the top of flights of stone steps, flanked by immense stone lions, and at the foot there was a statue of a man on a horse, one arm lifted up.

'*Energy*, the statue is called,' Jake said, as they walked down the steps. The whole memorial was so breathtaking, that Joanna could say nothing, could do no more than look around her wonderingly. Cape Town lay at their feet, and the sea sparkled blue behind it, with some huge container ships in the harbour and a few yachts out in the bay.

She was so taken up with looking at the city and the sea that she stumbled on the last step. Jake caught her, his arm strong around her. He was very close to her, so close that she could feel his breath warm on her cheek, his heart thudding so near her own.

And then his other arm was around her, too, and he was holding her even closer to him.

'I've wanted to do this for quite some time,' he murmured, and he kissed her, his lips warm on hers. Warm, and slowly becoming more demanding.

There was one moment when Joanna felt her whole body respond to him, when she felt her arms go around this big dark man, holding him even tighter to her.

And then, shocked and shaken by her own response, she drew back. Now there was no time to look for the right words. She just said it.

'I was at St Margaret's, too,' she said baldly, 'and I knew Helen. I saw her the day you broke your engagement to her. I saw how heartbroken she was.'

Jake's arms dropped to his sides.

'So that's it,' he said, very quietly. 'That's why you're so cool and distant. Because I'm a doctor who breaks nurses' hearts. Is that right?'

Joanna could only stare back at him defiantly.

'You'd made up your mind about me long ago, hadn't you?' he went on, almost conversationally. 'As soon as you recognised me, you were very sure you knew the kind of man I was. Isn't that so, Joanna Boyd?'

Joanna lifted her chin.

'Yes, it is,' she returned. Silently she added, Because I do. I knew someone just like you, someone I loved, someone I trusted. Someone who let me down just the way you let Helen down.

Unexpectedly, the big doctor smiled, but there was no warmth now in his blue eyes.

'And isn't it a lucky thing,' he said, 'that thinking you know what kind of man I am will protect you against the likes of me, girl dear? Just as it did a moment ago, when you kissed me.'

'It was you who kissed me,' Joanna flung back at him.

His eyes darkened. 'Then I must have been imagining the way you returned the kiss with interest, and the warmth there was when you put your arms around me, and when you held me just as close as I was holding you,' he murmured. 'Sure and it didn't seem that you had any objections to me kissing you.'

There was nothing Joanna could say to that. She stood on the step beside the stone lion, her head held high.

'I'll take you home,' Jake O'Connor said brusquely, and he turned and walked to where the car was parked, leaving her to follow him.

Neither of them said anything as he drove back down the winding, tree-lined road and turned onto the highway. To her horror, Joanna knew that she was very close to tears, and she was determined that the last thing she would do was let this man see her crying.

Jake drew up outside the old house.

I have to say something, Joanna thought.

'Thank you,' she managed to say, knowing her voice was less than steady.

He lifted one dark eyebrow.

'Now, that's an unnecessary thing to be saying, in the circumstances.'

He looked down at her, and in the confined space of the car there was nothing Joanna could do but sit very still, for her pride would not allow her to let him see that she was less than composed.

'I don't give a damn,' he said slowly, and very coldly, 'for your Victorian reaction to a broken engagement that is none of your business. What I do find decidedly unpleasant is that, without knowing me, without considering that there just might be two sides to the story, you made up your mind about me, you were quite sure that you had me taped. I don't like judgemental people and attitudes, Sister Boyd.'

He leaned over her, and opened the door.

'Thank you for accepting my invitation, Joanna,' he said, his hand still on the doorhandle, his dark head very close to her. 'Sure and I can see now, girl dear, that I would indeed be wasting this famous charm you've talked of, spending any more time with you.'

Other than the time we have to spend working together, Joanna thought bleakly as she pushed open the garden gate and walked up the path, hearing the brakes of the white sports car complain as the doctor turned and drove away.

None of her housemates were there, and she was glad of that, grateful for the cool silence of the old house around her as she made tea and sat on the swing seat on the stoep.

And slowly, reluctantly, she began to see that Jake O'Connor had been right. She had, indeed, made up her mind about him without knowing him. All right, there was still the memory of Helen, her eyes swollen, her face streaked with tears, but...he was right, she thought painfully. It's none of my business.

Except, she told herself, recovering a little, that he shouldn't be allowed to go around hurting people like that. Someone had to tell him, and I did. And I'm glad I did. I couldn't care less what he thinks of me, him and his talk of not wasting his charm on me. Thank you very much, Dr O'Connor, that will suit me very nicely.

But that night, in the cool darkness of her room, she found herself remembering his lips on hers, his body close to hers. And the way everything in her had responded to his kiss.

Electricity, she told herself firmly. Electricity, fascination. Whatever. Nothing more than that. No problem. The real problem was that they had to work together, and that could be difficult, after what had happened between them today.

Next day, at work, she realised that she needn't have worried. Jake O'Connor was completely professional, and no one, she was certain, could have guessed that the two of them had ever had any contact other than here in the hospital.

'Mrs September—Patience September—just booked in,' he said, looking at the charts in the duty room before Joanna and Sister Kenton accompanied him on his ward round. 'Isn't she the one who was advised to consider termination, with her history of renal disease?'

Sister Kenton nodded.

'It's against her religious belief,' she said, and for a moment her lips tightened. 'Even with your letter, saying that her condition could make pregnancy life-threatening. Dr Rajbansi saw her at the clinic last week and wanted her admitted now, early.'

Jake sighed.

'Right. We'll monitor her fluid balance, and restrict her dietary intake of sodium and potassium. And I'll monitor the foetal condition—our ultrasonic monitor will keep a constant check. That's all we can do to prevent her going into renal failure.'

'And if the blood urea or the serum potassium does rise too rapidly, dialysis therapy?' Joanna asked him, and he nodded.

'But we don't intend it to reach that stage,' he said firmly. His bleeper summoned him. 'I'll do that ward round later. Sister Kenton, Sister Boyd, she's in your capable hands. Call me if you have any problems.'

And with a nod, and a warm smile to Sister Kenton, he turned and left them.

'That young man has something on his mind, something bothering him,' the older woman said. 'Don't you think so, Sister Boyd?'

Joanna lifted the charts.

'I don't really know him, Sister,' she said carefully.

And that was true, she thought. All too true.

But if she didn't know Jake O'Connor—and didn't want to or need to, Joanna reminded herself firmly—she was beginning to know her housemates, and feeling more and more certain that the decision to share had been a good one.

Rose Hill was a year or two older than Joanna herself, and a quiet, thoughtful girl, with the same responsible attitude to her work that Joanna herself had. She was engaged to a young doctor, Andrew Morton, who had recently gone back to join his father in his practice in Kimberley.

'And as soon as we've saved a bit more we'll get married, and I'll get a post in the hospital there,' Rose told Joanna one morning when they were both off duty and had time to sit on their tiny stoep, having coffee.

'Why don't you go to Kimberley now?' Joanna asked. 'I know you miss him, and you could be together, even if you waited a bit to get married.'

Rose coloured, and Joanna had a fleeting thought that her name suited her well, with her fair hair and her skin now tinged pink.

'We want to have a proper wedding,' she said. 'My mother is on her own, and Andrew's folks haven't much, so we'll have to pay most of it ourselves. And they're pretty old-fashioned, my mum and Andrew's folks—they wouldn't be comfortable with us living together before that. So me being here and Andrew in Kimberley in some ways makes that easier.' She poured more coffee for each of them. 'Anyway, we'll have the rest of our lives together, and that's worth waiting for.'

It must be pretty good, Joanna thought soberly, to feel that way about someone. I never have, and maybe I never will. She remembered what she'd said to Dorothy about not being the romantic kind, about perhaps some day meeting someone she would get along well with, and that would be fine.

'You're miles away, Joanna,' Rose said. 'Thinking about someone?'

Joanna shook her head.

'No one to think about,' she replied truthfully. She patted her friend's hand. 'But don't worry. Trevor's taking me to the theatre on Friday, and next week I'm going to a party with David and Dorothy. So...you never know who I might meet there.'

'Yes, David and Dorothy,' Rose said thoughtfully. 'I rather think Dorothy is getting over her crush on Jake O'Connor, and looking closer to home. What do you think?'

'She'll do much better with David,' Joanna replied with conviction. 'I think Dr Jake O'Connor eats little girls like Dorothy for breakfast.'

She hadn't meant to sound quite so vehement, and she felt her cheeks grow warm as Rose looked at her, surprised and amused.

'And what about bigger girls like you?' she asked.

Joanna shook her head.

'Believe me, there's no chance of that—you know how I feel about doctors who think they're the answer to every nurse's prayer.'

'I can't say I see him like that,' Rose said slowly. 'I

think he just likes people—all right, women particularly—and he's naturally…'

She paused.

'Naturally charming?' Joanna suggested. She sniffed. 'I've seen him switch that charm on. He thinks that, and his Irish accent, gives him a free pass with any female.' She stood up. 'I'm using my day off to visit this famous Kirstenbosch,' she said. 'I don't know how interested I am in botanical gardens, but everyone says I have to go there. Want to come with me?'

Rose shook her head.

'Thanks, but I have letters to write and mending to do,' she said regretfully. 'But I agree, you must go to Kirstenbosch. If you walk to the far end, you'll see the wild almond hedge that Jan van Riebeeck planted. And there's a wonderful avenue of old camphor trees.'

Half an hour later, Joanna had to agree that the camphor avenue was worth seeing. The huge old trees cast their shade over the road, and she walked along it, glad that there weren't many people around, already feeling very much at peace. From the avenue of camphor trees she turned up a path beside a small stream, and there she found a wooden bench with a simple plaque on it, in memory of a young woman who had died five years ago. She sat there for a little while, wondering about this unknown young woman, about the husband and the daughters who had chosen this place to mark her memory.

And because there was still a raw ache in her heart for her mother, because somehow this huge garden made her think of her mother's small but cherished garden, she found herself weeping a little. But somehow there was something healing, she thought, about tears shed in a place like this.

She followed another path, remembering that Rose had

said to go and see the small bronze otter in a pool. And there he was, incredibly lifelike, on a rock, in the middle of the pool. A little girl was leaning precariously over the wall at the edge of the pool, and Joanna watched, amused, as the man with her lifted her back to safety.

'That's enough, Cathy,' he said, laughing. 'I'm not prepared to jump in and save you.'

Oh, no, Joanna thought, dismayed, as he swung round, the child in his arms. But there was no chance to retreat.

'Oh,' Jake O'Connor said flatly.

Yes, oh, indeed, Joanna thought, and she couldn't help a small rush of satisfaction at his obvious discomfort.

'It's very shallow and, anyway, I can swim,' the little girl said. She smiled at Joanna, a wide, gap-toothed smile. 'Do you and this lady know each other, Uncle Jake?'

Uncle Jake. Of course, Joanna thought, unwilling to examine her strange confusion at hearing this. Of course, she couldn't be his child.

She was about to say something, before turning and leaving the man and the child, when she saw, at the far end of the otter's pool, a young woman in a wheelchair. It was certainly the little girl's mother for they had the same fair curly hair, the same blue eyes. And the same smile, although rather more shy in the mother.

'Hello,' she said. 'Jake, do introduce me to your friend.'

The big doctor had recovered his composure now, and he set the child down on her feet.

'Alice, this is Joanna Boyd, she's a sister in Maternity Block.' His dark blue eyes met Joanna's, and she thought there was a touch of defiance on his lean brown face. 'She and I were at St Margaret's at the same time, although we didn't really know each other, did we, Joanna?'

Taking the war into the enemy's camp, Joanna thought, and daring me to take that any further.

She lifted her chin.

'No, we didn't, Jake,' she said, and she hoped her voice was as cool as his.

'Alice's husband is my cousin,' Jake said pleasantly, conversationally.

'And that's why he's my Uncle Jake,' the little girl, Cathy, told Joanna. ''Cos my Daddy and Uncle Jake were like brothers, much more than cousins, weren't you, Uncle Jake?'

Jake looked down at the child.

'That's right, Cathy,' he said.

'We're just going to have tea and scones, Joanna,' Alice said. 'Won't you join us? Tea and scones at Kirstenbosch is an institution. Isn't that so, Jake?'

Once again, there was a challenge in the doctor's eyes.

'Oh, yes,' he agreed. 'Kirstenbosch, Rhodes Memorial—you mustn't miss out on any experience like that, Joanna.'

How dare he? Joanna thought, furious. How dare he remind me?

And with her anger there was a strange bleakness that he could use that moment, that memory, like this—his arms around her, his lips warm on hers, warm and demanding. And her response, a response she would have given anything to forget.

Before she could say anything, make some excuse for refusing, the young woman in the wheelchair held out her hand.

'Please, come with us, Joanna,' she said.

And somehow Joanna found herself walking beside the wheelchair as Jake pushed it and Cathy ran ahead. Alice told her that she and Cathy lived in Stellenbosch, and they were here for Alice to keep a doctor's appointment.

'And we always come to see Uncle Jake when we come

to Cape Town,' Cathy said, coming back beside them. 'Can I have that big ice cream, Uncle Jake?'

'If your mother says you can,' Jake replied, as the small hand slipped into his. He smiled down at the child, and Joanna, in spite of herself, found the sight of the big, dark man and the child with her fair, curly hair, her small hand in his as they walked along, somehow disturbing. It didn't fit, somehow, with her picture of him.

As she and Jake had done before, they sat outside to have tea and scones, and Cathy's ice cream.

'It's a beautiful place,' Joanna said, looking at the rolling green lawns, the flower-beds, the trees and the bushes. And then she added, remembering what Rose had said, 'And I didn't even reach the wild almond hedge.'

'There are cycads, too, strange things, but fascinating,' Alice said. 'I haven't seen them for years—the path's too steep for my wheelchair.'

It was no more than a matter-of-fact comment, and she certainly wasn't looking for sympathy, but Joanna had to restrain an absurd impulse to cover Alice's hand with her own.

'I can see this will become a favourite place for me,' she said quickly. 'There are so many places I want to see, though. It's so beautiful, your Cape Town.'

'You haven't been here long, then?' Alice asked, and Joanna, taking herself by surprise, told her that she should have been here a year ago, but her plans had had to change because her mother had been ill.

'Is she better now?' Alice asked.

Joanna shook her head.

'She died,' she said quietly.

'Oh, Joanna, I'm so sorry,' Alice said, and her blue eyes filled with tears. 'My mother died six years ago. I do know how you must feel. You're very brave, coming to a new country, not clinging to familiar things.' She turned to Jake, and Joanna was disconcerted to see an expression that could be nothing but warm sympathy on his face. 'Jake, you must bring Joanna to visit us at the farm. When are you coming next? If you're off next weekend, and Joanna is, too, come and have lunch with us.'

'I'm not off next weekend,' Jake said quickly. He looked at Joanna, and in spite of her own dismay she couldn't help feeling a moment of amusement because he quite obviously felt equally dismayed.

'I'll leave you to fix it up, then,' Alice told Jake firmly. She looked at her small daughter. 'Cathy, you don't have to finish that ice cream, it's a very big one.'

'I was just thinking that,' the little girl agreed. 'Uncle Jake, would you like any of my ice cream? Would you, Joanna?' Reluctantly, she put her half-finished ice cream down on her mother's plate. 'Maybe next time I should have a smaller one.'

'Maybe you should,' Jake said. He looked at his watch. 'Alice, we should be moving—your appointment is in half an hour.'

He stood up purposefully and put his hands on Alice's wheelchair.

'We do have to hurry,' Alice said regretfully, 'but Jake will arrange things and bring you out to visit us, won't you, Jake?'

Joanna wondered if she was the only one to notice Jake's momentary hesitation or his somewhat forced smile.

'Of course, Alice,' he said. 'Come on, Cathy, race you to the car.' More formally he said, 'Goodbye, Joanna.'

'Goodbye,' Joanna returned, feeling all at once a little overwhelmed by the way this day had turned out.

She walked for a little longer in the beautiful gardens,

admiring the stone statues from Zimbabwe set out along the paths and on the lawns. She told herself that Jake felt just as she did, that any further contact between them was unwanted and unwelcome. He would manage to make some excuse to Alice, if she did press him to bring Joanna to visit her.

And yet she couldn't help a faint feeling of regret, for there had been something about the young woman in the wheelchair that she had really felt drawn to, something that had made her feel she would have liked to have got to know Alice better. But not if it meant any unnecessary contact with Jake O'Connor, she reminded herself.

Joanna hadn't expected that the brief encounter would make any difference to her working relationship with Jake, and she was glad to be proved right about that. He was always pleasant, but always completely professional.

And that's the way I want it, Joanna told herself when Jake had thanked her for the coffee she had made for him and confirmed that he would be back to check on one of his special patients later.

'You're very formal with each other, you and Jake,' Dorothy commented. 'I suppose that's your English training. He doesn't risk teasing you, and he even teases Sister Kenton sometimes.'

'I can live without being teased by Jake O'Connor,' Joanna said with complete truth.

'But I suppose that seems strange to you, him being Mr Wonderful himself?'

Dorothy thought about that.

'I do think he's an absolute dream,' she said after a moment. 'And I can go quite weak at the knees if he smiles at me, but maybe I wouldn't actually want to live with a dream. Maybe I could settle for someone a little more—more ordinary.'

'Like David, you mean?' Joanna couldn't resist asking.

Dorothy shrugged.

'Maybe. And maybe not. Anyway, you must admit he's a brilliant doctor. No, of course, I don't mean David, I mean Jake.'

'I know that,' Joanna agreed, for there was no doubt in her mind about that. The more she worked with Jake, the more her respect for him as a doctor grew.

She came back from her lunch-hour the next day to find Sister Kenton and Jake in the duty room, studying a chart.

'Ah, Sister Boyd,' Sister Kenton said, looking up. 'Dr O'Connor has just had a patient from the cardiac clinic admitted. Mrs Dladla. As soon as she's in second stage she'll be in your hands, so Dr O'Connor wants to go over the management of her labour with you.'

As Joanna walked along the corridor with Jake he ran rapidly over what he had arranged for his patient, who was in the first stage of labour.

'She's had diazepam to keep her calm, but I may have to prescribe morphine for pain,' he told her. 'We're avoiding over-hydration, and using a slow pump to control the IV fluid intake. I want you to watch for increased cyanosis and a pulse over 110.'

They had reached the end bed in the small side ward, and the brisk professional tone left his voice as he bent over the young black woman in the bed.

'Mrs Dladla,' he said, and the dark eyes opened. 'Sorry to disturb you when we've just got you feeling a little more comfortable, but I wanted you to meet Sister Boyd—she'll be looking after you.'

The young woman's eyes met Joanna's, and she tried to smile.

'Doctor says after this baby no more,' she said, and she tried to smile. 'We want this one to be a girl after the two boys, you see, Sister.'

Joanna patted her hand.

'We can't guarantee you a girl, Mrs Dladla,' she said, 'but we will certainly look after you and your baby.'

'Rest now,' Jake told his patient. 'I'll be in and out to see you.'

Outside the ward he looked down at Joanna, and his dark blue eyes were grave.

'She shouldn't be having this baby,' he said abruptly, 'but we've managed to look after her so far, and we're going to get this baby out safely, then we'll see what we can do for that heart of hers. Now, Sister Boyd, I want to be called as soon as she's in second stage, and we'll have Dr Wilson from the cardiac clinic here as well. Until we get Mrs Dladla there, this is what you do with her.

'She'll need continuous oxygen, and she must be allowed to take whatever position is most comfortable. She must not push—that heart will never stand it.' For a moment his face was bleak. 'Nor would it stand a Caesarean delivery. We'll shorten the perineal phase by doing an episiotomy, and then I'll use a vacuum extractor or do a low forceps delivery. We'll have an obstetric anaesthetist ready to give her nitrous oxide and oxygen. Got all that?'

Joanna nodded.

'I'll see to it, Dr O'Connor, and we'll send for you as soon as she is in second stage.'

'Thanks,' he said absently, for the first time without the usual professional formality. Because all his thoughts are with his patient, Joanna realised. He hardly knows it's me he's talking to. And she couldn't help admitting that was another good mark—in a completely professional sense—for Jake, to be totally absorbed with the young woman who needed his care.

A few hours later, when Mrs Dladla went into second stage, Joanna had her brought through to Labour Ward, and soon after that Jake and Dr Wilson arrived together.

'You're doing fine,' Jake told the young woman when he had examined her. 'I don't think this baby is going to be too long arriving.'

Which was just as well, Joanna knew, for she had seen the two doctors exchange a quick glance and she knew they weren't happy with the young woman's condition. Jake took the chance, while the older doctor was examining Mrs Dladla, to have a quick word with Joanna at the far side of the small theatre.

'I want packed cells ready in case she needs a blood transfusion, to avoid overloading the circulation,' he said, his voice low. 'And she'll need sedatives as soon as the baby is born.' He glanced across at the young woman in the bed. 'I'm sure you realise that the greatest danger is collapse when the retracted uterus returns blood to the general circulation. That can overload a heart like hers.'

Joanna had foreseen the need for packed cells, and she told him so.

Together they went back to their patient. She had been given a mild anaesthetic, and was extremely drowsy.

'This baby has got to be born now, Jake,' Dr Wilson said, when he had checked the monitor for her heart again. 'And I mean *now*.'

Jake nodded.

'I'll do a low forceps delivery,' he said, 'with an episiotomy—the head is far enough down.'

Joanna had worked with him often enough to be able to anticipate the instruments he needed, and each time he stretched out his hand she was ready. Gently, expertly, he applied the forceps to the baby's head and drew the squirming little bundle out.

The staff nurse was ready to take the baby, but Joanna saw in one swift glance that Mrs Dladla had got her little girl.

Jake's eyes met hers.

'The baby is safe,' he said tersely. 'Now we have to make sure the mother is, too. And that's what we're going to do.'

Two of the best doctors in the huge hospital, Joanna thought. And me.

And in spite of her anxiety about the patient, she couldn't help a moment of pride at being part of this team.

CHAPTER THREE

THERE was a swift consultation between the two doctors, and Jake gave the young mother an injection of ergometrine so that the uterus would contract and stop bleeding.

'We can't risk severe blood loss,' he said, his eyes on the monitor, as Dr Wilson's were. Joanna, intent on their patient, could only look when the stitching was finished.

'What do you think?' Jake said to Dr Wilson.

'I think we've got away with it,' the older man said quietly. 'She's stable now.' He turned to Joanna. 'And the baby?'

Joanna turned to the staff nurse.

'I've suctioned her, and her Apgar score is eight,' the nurse told them.

'Pretty good,' Jake said to Joanna, and he smiled. 'Considering the mother's condition. Let's have a look at her.'

The baby was tiny in his hands, but she lay still as if she felt the confidence and the security of the hands holding her. And once again Joanna had that strange, disturbing feeling, a feeling that she was beginning to admit was a questioning, a longing, that came over her each time she saw a newborn baby. The big Irish doctor looked down at the baby, and Joanna felt that she was seeing something more that threw all her perceptions of this man. He looked up, and for a moment smiled at her, a smile that held all the shared triumph of what they had just achieved. Joanna, filled with that as well, returned his smile.

And then, as if a barrier had come down, the warmth left Jake's eyes, and he turned away.

'We'll have her in the ICU for a few hours, Adam,' he said to the older doctor. 'Then we can move her to Cardiac. How soon can you operate, do you think?'

They moved towards the door together, their voices too low to be heard by the young woman in the bed, who was still barely conscious.

'I'd like to operate on her within a few days, if she can take it,' Dr Wilson said. 'I think a bypass could change her quality of life—give her a chance of seeing this little one grow up.'

They went out of the room, but Jake turned back.

'I'll be in to check on Mrs Dladla as soon as I've done my rounds,' he said, 'but buzz me if you need me any sooner, Sister Boyd.' He hesitated. 'Thanks—you did a good job.'

Brusque, awkward, but praise from him did mean something. Because he's so darned good, Joanna told herself as she and her staff nurse cleaned their patient up and wheeled her along to the ICU. Dr Wilson had arranged for one of his cardiac nurses to special her there, and the baby would be kept in the nursery.

Just as they were leaving her, the young mother's eyes opened.

'My baby?' she asked anxiously.

'Your baby is fine, Mrs Dladla,' Joanna told her. 'And you've got your little girl. I'll bring her along and let you see her.

'And we'll do that,' she told her staff nurse as they went back along the corridor, 'before she's told about her operation. I'm a firm believer in doing everything possible to help patients to have a positive approach.'

Suddenly, now that the drama of the delivery was over, she realised that she was exhausted. She had just poured herself a cup of coffee when Jake came in.

'You look as bad as I feel,' she said, without stopping to remind herself that this was exceeding the limits of professional formality, for his dark eyes were shadowed and there were lines of strain around his mouth. She poured coffee for him.

'Thanks,' he said, and he sat down. 'Yes, I thought we were going to lose her. I've never done a delivery when the mother's heart was in such a bad condition.'

He drank his coffee and leaned back, his hands behind his head and his eyes closed. Joanna, watching, had a ridiculous impulse to put a cushion behind that dark head, to put a stool under his feet.

He opened his eyes to find her looking at him, and she felt warm colour flood her cheeks. Hastily, she put her cup down.

'I must get back to the ward,' she said, knowing she sounded awkward, ill at ease.

'Yes, I really just came back to tell Mrs Dladla about her baby, but she was asleep. But Sister Jones said you had told her.'

He stood up, and Joanna went to the door with him, telling him that she would take the baby along soon to let her mother see her.

'Yes, do that,' he said. 'She'll go into the operation in a good frame of mind.'

He strode off down the corridor, his white coat flying, and Joanna, as she went back to the busy ward, couldn't help thinking that these moments when both he and she had forgotten the hostility between them made working together very much more pleasant.

But the formality and the professional distance were back by the next day, and although Jake reported on the successful bypass operation Dr Wilson had performed on Mrs Dladla, he did it without any indication that he remembered that shared drama, that closeness which had come with working together to save two lives.

Not that I want anything but a good working relationship, Joanna reminded herself more than once as she stood beside Jake while he examined a new patient. And we do have that.

A day or two later, when she went off duty, as she was waiting for the lift, Jake came hurrying along the corridor.

'I thought I'd missed you,' he said. 'Surely you're late going off duty?'

'Yes, I am,' Joanna replied. 'Handing over sometimes takes a while, depending on how busy the ward is. Did you want to check on Mrs Brenton? She's only just in second stage, so I told Sister Harris she should let you know when—'

She stopped, as he shook his dark head.

'Actually, it's nothing to do with the ward. I wanted to see you,' he said brusquely. 'I'll walk down the road with you.'

He got into the lift beside her and pressed the button. Joanna was all too conscious of many curious glances as she and Jake walked out of the hospital together. As they headed down the hill towards the main road he said, without looking at her, 'I had a phone call from Alice last night. She wants me to fix a date, and bring you out to see her. Are you off this weekend?'

Joanna stopped.

'Yes, I am,' she said. And then, more baldly than she had meant to, she went on, 'But you don't really want to do this, and—'

'And neither do you,' Jake finished for her.

There was no need to feel defensive, Joanna told herself, but undoubtedly she did.

'It was very kind of Alice,' she said quickly, 'and I

really would have liked to see her again, but…' Once again, she stopped.

'But not if it means involving me,' Jake said.

Joanna walked on, quickly now, in spite of the lingering heat of the day, but the big man's long, easy strides matched hers effortlessly.

'You don't want that any more than I do,' she pointed out.

'No, I don't,' he agreed. 'But you must realise that Alice's life is far from easy. She's always been a shy person, and it's even more difficult for her to reach out to people now. This is the first time since her accident that I've known her do something like this. If you refuse to go and see her, she'll find it very hard to try again. So, on that basis, could we set our personal feelings aside, and let me take you to visit her?'

They had reached the main road, and as they waited for the traffic lights to change, Joanna knew that she couldn't refuse. She turned to Jake.

'All right, I'll come,' she said flatly. 'You don't need to come any further with me.'

'Yes, I do,' he returned, as the little green man appeared. He put his hand on her arm, and hurried her across the busy road. 'You have to be quick, the green man doesn't allow for anything but a mad dash,' he told her, as they reached the opposite pavement just in time. 'I'll pick you up on Sunday morning at nine. Bring your bathing costume, we'll probably swim.'

Joanna could see Dorothy watering the tiny garden. Any minute now, she would look up and see them. Yes, she had. She waved, and Joanna waved back. Jake waved as well.

'I'll be ready,' Joanna said quickly. If it had been anyone but him, she would have asked him to come to the house for coffee or a beer, but not Jake. Anyway, he wouldn't want to draw this interchange out any longer, she was certain.

'Joanna,' he said, abruptly, 'your friends in the house—do they know that we knew each other at St Margaret's?'

'Oh, yes,' Joanna told him, and she had the satisfaction of seeing dismay in his blue eyes. 'But I wouldn't say we knew each other. I knew you, that's all.' Then, because she had an uneasy feeling that she was being a little childish, she said quietly, 'I haven't told anyone about Helen, and you needn't worry, I have no intention of doing so.'

It was a moment before he said anything.

'You may find this hard to believe.' His voice was steady, and so were the dark eyes looking down into hers. 'I'm not too concerned about that, I just wanted to know. You see, people here will judge me on my merits—they aren't likely to hear one side of a story and decide on the kind of man I am on the basis of that. See you on Sunday.'

Joanna didn't watch him walk away, but when she reached the house Dorothy was standing with the hose in her hand and a bed of roses overflowing at her feet.

'He walked you home,' she said breathlessly, as Joanna took the hose firmly from her and moved it to the huge frangipani at the side of the stoep. 'Why didn't you ask him in?'

'He was in a hurry,' Joanna told her untruthfully. 'Anyway, he wouldn't have wanted to come. He was just making arrangements for Sunday.'

Dorothy's eyes were wide.

'You're going out with Jake?'

Joanna sighed. She explained about meeting his cousin's wife at Kirstenbosch, and Alice wanting her to come and visit.

'It isn't a date or anything like that,' she pointed out. 'It's no big deal, Dorothy.'

She turned the water off.

'Doesn't the frangipani smell wonderful at this time, when it's just been watered?' she said.

'I can take a hint,' her friend returned. 'No more talking about Jake. But, oh, I wish I wasn't working on Sunday, I'd love to see how you get ready to go out on a date that isn't a date, with a man like that! Come on, now, you have to admit he's definitely an absolute honey. So good-looking, and I could just melt when I see that smile. Have you decided what you're going to wear?'

'Not a problem,' Joanna said airily. And it wasn't, because while she'd been doing the watering she'd already decided that she would wear her new kingfisher blue dress of Indian cotton because it was nice and cool. And Stellenbosch, she had heard, could be even hotter than Cape Town.

Chosen for its coolness, the dress did look nice, she thought as she looked at herself in the mirror just before nine on Sunday morning. And her own appreciation was mirrored in Jake's as she got into the car. He did seem determined to stick to what he had said about leaving personal feelings aside, and as they talked about the hospital, and about Cape Town, Joanna found, to her surprise and relief, that it was certainly possible to do that.

But at the same time she couldn't help being conscious of a stiffness, a formality, which she knew there wouldn't have been between a man like Jake and a girl he was taking out for the day, if she hadn't said the things she had.

It wasn't only what I said, it was the way I said it, she thought with honesty. And with that same honesty she realised, Perhaps he's right, perhaps I did judge him too quickly. But it was too late to think that way and, anyway, there was the memory of Helen Johnson, her face tear-stained, her eyes red. Jilted by Jake O'Connor. An old-fashioned word, but the right one, Joanna reminded herself.

'The mountains are beautiful, aren't they?' Jake said, and Joanna, glad to be jolted out of her thoughts, agreed. The sky was clear and blue above the small country town they were approaching, and there was a blue haze on the mountains rising behind it.

'Cloud building up behind the mountains,' Jake observed. 'The forecast did say we could have a storm later. Don't worry, they're often wrong. This is a university town,' he told her, as he pointed out the old Cape Dutch houses lining wide streets, shady with the oak trees Stellenbosch was, he said, famous for. As they passed jeans-clad young people, cycling along, he added, 'And small enough for bicycles to be the accepted transport. Not as many students, of course. Most of them have finished for the year.'

'Of course,' Joanna said. 'The school and university year will run from January to December, because this is the long summer holiday. Neater, somehow, than the way we have it.'

They passed a wide, grassy square, with a tiny old church at the far side, and then Jake drove out of the town, and into the vine-clad hills. He turned into a side road, winding through fields of ripening grapes.

'What does the name mean—Morgenster?' she asked him. 'Did I say it right?'

'Not bad,' he said. 'It means Morning Star, in Afrikaans. Here we are.'

The house was wide and sweeping, with a thatched roof

and a wide verandah—a stoep, she reminded herself—running round three sides of it. And a huge garden, beautifully tended. Jake drew up at the steps leading to the front door. Alice, from her wheelchair, waved to them, her face alight. Cathy, her small body golden brown against the bright red of the bathing costume she was wearing, ran down the steps, a large golden dog beside her.

'Uncle Jake, I've been waiting for you for hours,' she said, and she ran into the big doctor's waiting arms. He lifted her up and hugged her, and then, with the little girl still in his arms, he bent and kissed her mother's cheek.

Alice held out one hand to Joanna.

'I'm so glad you could come, Joanna,' she said. 'I know it's difficult, getting your weekend off at the same time, but I've been looking forward so much to you coming.'

'This is Simba,' Cathy told Joanna. 'Simba, shake hands with Joanna.'

Solemnly, the big dog held out a paw, and Joanna, equally solemnly, shook it.

'Simba means lion,' Cathy said confidentially, 'but he's actually a golden retriever.'

'He's beautiful,' Joanna said. 'We had a Labrador at home, my mother and I. He was golden, too.'

'Simba likes people who know you should shake hands with a dog,' Cathy said approvingly. 'So do I.'

Ridiculously, Joanna felt a warm glow at the child's approval and, even more ridiculously, a glow when she saw that the stiffness had gone from Jake's face. His dark blue eyes were laughing as the big dog held out a paw to him, and his lean, brown face creased in a smile.

'Cathy, ask Anna to bring coffee for us, would you?' Alice said. She turned to Jake as the child and the dog ran inside the house. 'Philip won't be long, Jake, he had to pick up some papers from the office. My husband is a lawyer,' she said to Joanna.

Joanna looked at the vineyards that surrounded the house.

'As well as being a farmer?' she asked.

Alice shook her head.

'This was my father's farm. Philip doesn't know anything about growing grapes—we have a farm manager.'

A large woman came out, carrying a tray, and Alice deftly pushed herself to the table and poured coffee. The big golden dog, who seemed to have taken a fancy to Joanna, leaned his head on her knee.

'Cupboard love,' Jake said, smiling. 'He's seen these crunchies on the tray, although he knows he's not allowed to be fed at the table. Push him away, Joanna, if he's a nuisance.'

'He isn't,' Joanna replied. She patted the dog's head, and his plumed tail wagged in appreciation. 'I love having him sit like this. Our Shandy used to do the same.'

She hadn't realised that her face had given her away, but Alice leaned forward and for a moment her hand covered Joanna's.

'And you miss him,' she said softly.

Joanna nodded, her throat all at once tight.

'The people who bought our house took him,' she said. 'I had a letter a few weeks ago. He seems to have settled down with them—they're retired, and they take him for long walks in the wood so he's quite happy. But, yes, I miss him.'

Cathy, having finished her orange juice, perched on Jake's knee.

'Would you like to see my tree-house, Uncle Jake?' she asked him. 'It's the one you helped me to build last summer, but I've been rearranging it.'

Jake put his cup down, and assured her that he would certainly like to see it.

The two young women watched the man and the child and the dog walk across the wide lawn, Cathy's small hand in Jake's.

'I worry about her, being an only child,' Alice said quietly. 'I was as well, but I had cousins around me. Just as Jake and Philip had each other. They grew up together, you know, and they've always been close, like brothers.'

For a moment there was a shadow in her blue eyes, and Joanna thought she changed her mind about what she was going to say.

'It was Philip's idea to ask Jake to come out here,' she said. 'That was after he and his fiancée Helen—you'll know about that, of course.'

Oh, yes, Joanna thought, I know. And if I needed to be reminded that Jake has another side from this kind uncle, the man dogs and children like, this has done it.

'Yes,' she said. 'Yes, I do know about that.'

Alice sighed.

'Jake never talks about it, and I don't like to ask, but I think the whole thing hurt him very deeply.'

Yes, Joanna thought, and it hurt Helen very deeply, too. I know all about a hurt like that because I've also been there.

But she didn't say anything, and after a moment Alice waved to Jake and Cathy, coming back across the lawn.

'Push me down the ramp, Joanna, would you?' she said. 'And bring your bag with you—you have brought a costume, I hope.' She glanced at the sky, and Joanna saw to her surprise that the clouds were building up. 'You can have a swim before lunch in case we do get rain.'

There was a small changing room beside the pool, and Joanna changed there, wishing all at once that she had brought her other costume, which was a little more substantial than the bikini she now looked at doubtfully. It had seemed all right in the shop, but there wasn't a great deal of it.

'I like bikinis,' Cathy said approvingly, when she went out. 'I usually wear one, but I want to show you how I can dive, and you can't dive very well in a bikini, can you?'

'No, you can't,' Joanna agreed. 'But I don't plan on doing much diving, Cathy.'

'Just as well,' Jake said, and there was warm laughter in his voice. And, Joanna realised, considerable appreciation on his face.

But only for a moment. Then it was gone, and the cool distance was back. And Joanna was thrown to realise how much she wished that things were different between herself and this man. In spite of everything she knew about him, everything she felt about him.

Perhaps it was because of the confusion of her own feelings, Joanna thought later, that she was conscious of some hint of strain between Jake and his cousin Philip.

Philip Sullivan, although he also had a hint of an Irish accent, didn't look at all like Jake. Brown hair, grey eyes, and not as tall as Jake. He greeted Joanna courteously, and when they went onto the stoep to have lunch at the table set out in the shade, he asked about her preference for wine.

'I don't know a great deal about South African wines,' Joanna admitted. 'What do you like, Alice?'

'Let's have some of the Nederburg Rosé,' Alice said. She explained that they didn't make their own wine, but supplied nearby wine-makers with grapes, and were then given a quota of the wine.

The cold chicken, other cold meats and salads were

perfect in the heat of the day—a heat that became more oppressive and had Jake looking at the build-up of clouds. They had just finished coffee when there was a low rumble of thunder.

'I think we'd better head back to Cape Town,' Jake said. 'Sorry to cut short our visit, but I don't fancy driving through a real storm. Is that all right with you, Joanna?'

Joanna had been hoping that no one had seen her reaction to the thunder. Since she'd been a child she'd had this fear of storms.

'Yes, of course,' she agreed. It was less than an hour's drive and they might get back before the storm broke.

'But you will come back soon, Joanna?' Alice asked. 'Next time Jake comes, perhaps.'

For a moment, the big doctor's eyes met Joanna's, and there was a question in them. A question, and a plea.

I can't say yes unless I mean it, Joanna thought. Not to Alice. And little Cathy.

'Thanks, Alice, I'd like that,' she said, adding, to give both herself and Jake some manoeuvring room, 'Of course, we don't always have the same time off, so it might not be too easy.'

'But you will come,' Alice said, and Joanna nodded.

They walked across the lawn to Jake's car, and she found herself with Philip.

'I hope we do see you soon, Joanna,' he said, taking her by surprise for he sounded as if he really meant it. He smiled a little diffidently. 'You had Alice laughing today when you told that story about when you were a student nurse and you got shut in the broom cupboard. It was good to hear her laugh again.'

If Joanna had had any doubts about her promise to come back with Jake, Philip's words settled that.

As they drove off down the tree-lined drive, between

the vineyards, she turned to wave to Cathy, who was jumping up and down as she waved, the big golden dog beside her.

'Thank you for coming, Joanna,' Jake said quietly, as he turned onto the main road. 'It was good to hear Alice laughing.'

'Philip said that, too,' Joanna told him. She hesitated, unwilling to get into anything other than careful social small talk, but she did want to know. 'How long has Alice been in a wheelchair?'

'Two years,' Jake said. He hesitated, too, but only for a moment. 'They were coming back home one evening when a tractor came out of a farm road. Philip tried to avoid it, by swerving, and the car turned over. He...blames himself for the accident, but I don't think he could have done anything else. It was just one of those awful things. At least Cathy wasn't with them.'

She would have liked to have asked more about the medical details of Alice's injuries, but in the darkening sky ahead of them there was a flash of sheet lightning and then an unbelievably loud rumble of thunder. Joanna, unable to stop herself, gasped.

Jake glanced at her.

'I'm afraid we're going to be caught in this,' he said, and the even tone of his voice helped her to regain her composure. 'We don't get too many summer storms in the Cape, but I'm afraid this one is building up for a real good one.'

'A good one?' Joanna repeated. Although she had tried to speak lightly, her voice shook.

Now there was forked lightning as well as sheet, and the rain began with the next crack of thunder. Jake pulled off the road.

'I think we'll sit this one out,' he said.

The rain beat on the roof of the car, and the thunder rolled around them. Joanna could feel her heart thudding with fear and her forehead was damp. The last thing she wanted was for Jake to see this, but there was no way she could hide it from him.

'You don't like storms?' he said.

Joanna shook her head wordlessly.

'I'm not mad about storms myself, so we'll just keep each other company, I think.'

He put his arms around her and held her close. As if I'd been a child, Joanna thought later. A frightened child who'd had to be comforted. Gradually, the warmth and the security of his arms stilled her fear.

There was another bright fork of lightning across the heavy clouds, and a clap of thunder, and without giving herself time to think she buried her face against Jake's shoulder.

His arms tightened around her.

'That was further away,' he told her, and she could feel his breath warm on her hair. 'I think the worst of it is over.'

And it was. The jagged forks of lightning were further away, and the thunder was fading in the distance. Slowly, Joanna began to recover. And to be very conscious that she was in Jake's arms, her face buried against his shoulder.

She drew back, out of the circle of his arms.

'Thank you,' she said, stiffly. 'I—I've always been such a coward with storms. I'm sorry to have behaved so foolishly.'

Then a dreadful thought struck her, and she looked up at him.

'I hope you don't think I was just…'

She wasn't sure how to go on, but he did it for her.

'Pretending, so that I would have to do what I just did?' His amusement was natural and genuine, and at that moment there was no hostility in the way he looked down at her. 'Girl dear, you would have to be an Academy Award actress to put on a show like that. Oh, no, I never for a moment thought that you were pretending.'

He was still very close to her, and his blue eyes were very dark as he looked down at her. Joanna felt very conscious of the uneven thudding of her heart. Not from fear of the storm now, but because of the nearness of this man in the small enclosed world of the car, with the rain beating down on the roof.

She never knew, when she thought about it afterwards, which one of them moved first. She thought perhaps he said her name once, his voice low and not quite steady. And then his lips were on hers, urgent, demanding, and there was nothing she could do but return his kiss, with the same urgent response of her whole body.

It was Jake who had drawn back, and each time afterwards she thought of that her cheeks were warm with shame.

'I shouldn't have done that,' he said abruptly. 'I'm sorry.'

It was a moment before she could reply, and she was all too conscious that her voice was less than steady.

'It was just as much my fault,' she said. She took a deep, steadying breath. 'So…can we just forget it happened?'

For one moment there was something extremely disturbing in his eyes, and then it was gone.

'Of course,' he agreed, and there was some small satisfaction for Joanna in realising that his voice, like her own, wasn't quite steady.

Neither of them said much the rest of the way home.

Joanna was grateful that Jake made no reference to that unexpected and bewildering kiss when they parted.

Can we just forget it happened? she had said to him. Disturbingly, she found herself wondering if he was finding that as hard to do as she was.

Of course, as she had known it would be, there was no change in their working relationship. It was as if neither that moment in the car nor, in fact, the day spent together had happened. And I'm grateful for that, Joanna sensibly reminded herself more than once.

Every day on Labour Ward was busy, and a lull could be deceptive. A few days later, with three patients in second stage, and only one likely to have an immediate delivery, suddenly all three babies had to be delivered within twenty minutes, and Joanna and her staff nurse had to hurry to restore their ward to a state of readiness for the next delivery.

'Now we're ready to be in business again,' Joanna said, when they had finished. 'We may be in luck, though, barring emergencies. Things seem fairly quiet.'

'Sister Boyd?'

Unable to prevent a warm flood of colour to her face, Joanna turned towards the door.

'Yes, Dr O'Connor?'

Steady and professional I sound, she told herself.

'We've managed to keep Mrs September and her renal problems stabilised long enough to give the baby a good chance,' he said, 'but her serum potassium level is rising, and she's feeling pretty ill. I don't want to risk waiting any longer. She's a multipara, so I'm hoping to get away with an induction, not a Caesarean. Set up a pitocin drip and keep me in touch, will you?'

Patience September was over thirty, with two children,

and although she had managed to keep cheerful through the days she had been kept in hospital she was nervous now, Joanna could see, as well as feeling ill.

'Having my tubes tied after this one, Sister,' she said. 'It's no joke, looking after two small kids when you're feeling like I did before Dr O'Connor brought me in. Thank heavens for my mum. She's looking after them, and she'll help when I get home with this one.'

'Not surprising you didn't feel great, Mrs September,' Joanna said, adjusting the drip so that it flowed smoothly. 'Kidney problems are bad at any time, but especially in pregnancy.'

'I've got a boy and a girl, so it doesn't matter what this one is,' her patient told her. Then, for a moment, her voice was unsteady. 'Just so long as it's all right. I didn't really plan on having a third one, but I've kind of got used to the idea over these months and I wouldn't like anything to...' Her voice trailed off.

Joanna straightened, and smiled reassuringly.

'Your baby's doing fine, Mrs September, and there's a good strong heartbeat. We'll send for Dr O'Connor as soon as you're in second stage—he wants to be here with you.'

Within an hour it was time to send for Jake, and he hadn't been there long when the baby was born, a quicker, easier birth than Joanna had expected. Seeing the relief in the doctor's eyes, she knew that he'd had the same thoughts.

She wrapped up the healthily yelling baby boy, and put him in his mother's arms.

'Sounds just as noisy as his brother did,' their patient murmured.

'He's certainly got a good pair of lungs on him,' Jake agreed. 'Mrs September, I'm taking you back to the renal ward for a bit—your baby will be in the nursery, but he'll be brought to you. We need to keep a pretty careful eye on you.'

Half an hour later, when Joanna had just finished checking that her induction tray was once again ready for use, he looked round the door.

'Just wanted to tell you that we've got her on dialysis,' he said. 'But she's going to be all right. And her husband has agreed to the tubal ligation so there won't be a problem. She's keen to start feeding as soon as she's off dialysis. Can you have one of your nurses take the baby to her when they let you know?'

Briskly, professionally, he nodded when Joanna said she would see to that, and strode off along the corridor.

I can't fault him as a doctor in any way at all, Joanna thought, not for the first time. He's good, he's caring, he's compassionate.

So how come he can be so different as a man? she wondered, also not for the first time. Because he certainly hadn't been any of these things to the girl he had been engaged to. And then, disconcertingly, there was the memory of the way he had held her and comforted her in the storm.

I don't understand this man at all, Joanna thought. But then, I don't need to. He's a doctor I work with, and that is all.

Christmas was only a few weeks away, and the shops were full of Christmas decorations and the sound of Christmas carols.

'And if there's anything more ridiculous than listening to Bing Crosby dreaming of a white Christmas when the sun is shining from a cloudless sky and the temperature is almost thirty, I can't think of it,' Joanna said to Rose when they were both off duty one day. 'Not to mention "Sleigh Ride"!'

'You'll have to get used to it,' Rose pointed out mildly. 'This is the way Christmas is here. So are you off to the shops, or is it too much of a culture shock for you?'

Joanna shook her head.

'No, I'm going to do some Christmas shopping in the shop at Kirstenbosch. I haven't been to that wild almond hedge yet, so I can perhaps do that, too.'

The big, airy shop was cool and pleasant, and she found a pretty teapot for Rose, two attractive pottery mugs for Dorothy and, with a smile to herself, another two for David, for it was beginning to look as if he and Dorothy were becoming more than housemates.

And now, she decided, a cup of coffee before I tackle that walk.

Christmas, she thought as she stirred her coffee, and now the pleasure of finding the right presents for her friends was gone. The first Christmas without her mother. It wasn't going to be too easy when she remembered other Christmases at the cottage, the Christmas tree in the corner beside the window, the curtains drawn against the cold, the fire burning brightly and the old dog blissfully asleep in front of it. And her mother's face, thin last year but bright, over the candles on the table.

Her eyes blurred with tears, and her throat was tight. Unseeing, she put her cup down on the table.

'Joanna?'

Jake stood beside her, and the usual polite formality on his face was gone. Even through the blur of tears Joanna could see his concern.

'Are you all right?' he said, and he sat down.

'Yes— No— It's just...'

It was the sympathy in his voice, in his eyes, Joanna told herself. She found herself telling him, rather unsteadily, that she had just been thinking how difficult Christmas was going to be.

'It isn't even going to feel like Christmas when it's hot and sunny,' she said sadly.

Had it really happened, she wondered later, or had she just imagined that for one brief moment Jake's hand had covered hers on the table?

'Maybe that's not such a bad thing,' he suggested. 'This first Christmas without your mother—it's going to be so different, so unlike any Christmas you've known, that might make it just a little less hard.'

Joanna thought about that.

'You could be right,' she said. And then, ill at ease because he had seen her so vulnerable, she said, a little awkwardly, that she was going to walk to the wild almond hedge.

'I'll come with you,' Jake said, taking her by surprise.

'You don't have to do that,' she told him defensively.

Disconcertingly, there was amusement in the dark blue eyes.

'No, I don't,' he agreed. 'But, dear girl, if I have a fancy to walk to the wild almond hedge, and so do you, does it not seem foolish for us not to do that together?'

For a moment he was serious again.

'It's a lovely day, and I could see you were feeling a bit low. Just for a little while, could we perhaps forget that there's some bad feeling between us, on your side and on mine, and...just have a walk together?'

I don't know what to make of this man, Joanna thought, bewildered. He shouldn't be doing this, being kind, being perceptive—not the man I thought he was. And then, correcting herself, the man I know he is.

Jake stood up, and Joanna stood up, too.

'You don't have to do this because you're sorry for me,' she said.

'For heaven's sake,' he returned, exasperated, 'are you as prickly as this with everyone, or is it just me? Put that hat on your head, and come along.'

Joanna, rather to her own surprise, found herself following him as he strode out of the coffee-shop, stopping only to pay. It didn't seem a good idea, she thought, to make a fuss right now about paying for her own coffee.

Jake slowed down as they walked up one of the broad paths, heading upwards. He pointed out to her in each flower-bed the name of the gardener who looked after it.

'And this is the garden for the blind,' he told her, leading her along a small side path. 'Braille on the notices, and everything has a wonderful aromatic smell. There's a walk on the other side of the path with a rope to hold onto and information in braille at each interesting point. When I came here first, Philip and Alice and I brought Cathy here and made her close her eyes and walk, holding onto the rope, so that she would know what it felt like to be blind.'

They walked on, past the pool with the bronze otter where they had met by chance before. It seemed possible now to ask him more about Alice.

'Can nothing be done for her?' she said. 'Is the damage irreversible?'

Jake sighed.

'There is an operation that has a reasonable chance of success,' he told her, 'and there's at least one neurosurgeon in Cape Town who can do it. I've spoken to him and shown him Alice's X-rays and her reports, and he's willing to take a chance and operate.'

'So why doesn't Alice go ahead?' Joanna asked.

'It isn't that simple,' he replied. 'After the accident, with the various tests being done, Alice's ECG showed up as abnormal. Her heart isn't as bad as to need treatment but risky for an operation as lengthy as this would be, perhaps.'

'And she doesn't want to risk it, of course,' Joanna said. 'Better to be in a wheelchair than take a chance.'

Jake stopped, and she was glad for the path had become quite steep.

'We're almost there,' he said. 'Look at that view of Cape Town spread out between the mountain and the sea. Isn't it stunning?'

The sea shimmered in the heat, blue and calm, and the mountain rose imposingly above the sprawling city. It certainly was stunning, Joanna agreed.

'Let's sit down before we tackle the last stretch,' Jake said, and they sank onto a wooden bench which also had a plaque on it in memory of someone else who must have loved this place.

'What I want,' he said abruptly, 'is for Alice to have an angiogram to determine just what the damage to her heart is, and to let us all evaluate the risks of an operation. But Philip won't agree, and for some reason Alice won't take a stand against him.'

Joanna thought about that.

'It's an invasive procedure, an angiogram,' she said, 'and, of course, there is some risk.'

He stood up.

'Alice says it's because he almost lost her once, and he can't bear to risk that again.'

Alice says? Joanna looked at him, a question in her eyes.

'He hasn't talked about it to me,' he said, his voice level. 'I've tried, but it's no use.'

And yet Alice had said they'd been so close when they'd been young. But there was a shadow in Jake's blue eyes, a tightness about his mouth, that stopped her asking any more.

'Let's get to the wild almond hedge,' he said, 'before the day gets any hotter.'

He held out his hand, and Joanna, without stopping to think, put her own hand into his.

CHAPTER FOUR

AS SWIFTLY as she had done it, Joanna drew her hand back from Jake's, all too conscious of a flood of colour in her cheeks. And of amusement in the dark blue eyes looking down at her.

Amusement, and nothing more, she realised wonderingly. No coolness, no hostility, no distance. Just two people sharing a pleasant summer morning walk.

The wild almond hedge wasn't much to see, she had to admit, but she liked the sense of history about being there, at what had once been the outside limit of the early settlement here in Table Bay.

'Cape of Storms, it was called,' Jake reminded her as they walked down towards the wide lawns again. 'And sailors still know all about that. Last summer an oil rig broke free from its moorings and crashed around other ships until it came to rest in a corner of the harbour.'

They went on to talk about the hospital until they reached the car park, and Jake's concern at necessary cost-cutting measures. Another side I don't know to this man, Joanna thought, a little dazed as he spoke of staff shortages, cut-backs in surgical procedures and two theatres being closed down. It wasn't easy to remember that this was the same man who had reduced a girl she knew, a confident, beautiful girl, to that poor heartbroken girl in the garden.

When this thought came to her again a few days later, it was followed by another, even more disturbing thought. Why was it so important to her to remember that? Did it really matter when she weighed it against the man she had come to know? And yet—and yet—for some reason that she didn't care to examine too closely she did need to remind herself of it. Because he was so like Cliff. Because he'd treated Helen the way Cliff had treated her.

I just couldn't ever trust him, she told herself with clarity. All right, there is this strange…chemistry, electricity, whatever, that I feel when I'm with him. So perhaps I just have to be very careful of that, and very conscious of it. And not forget what I know about him.

In spite of the warmer relationship between them, as they worked together she would occasionally find his eyes resting on her, cool, assessing, and she would know, with a sudden heaviness of her heart, that he was reminding herself of the way she had prejudged him, had made up her mind about him so completely.

So it's a truce, nothing more, she told herself. And that was all right because she didn't want anything more from him, and she was quite sure he wanted nothing more from her.

Maternity Block seemed to be busier and busier as the days passed before Christmas.

'It's that cold snap we had in early March,' Dorothy said cheerfully. 'And it looks as if we're going to be even busier.'

She had moved from the ICU, and was now Joanna's staff nurse. We work well together, Joanna often thought in these busy days, grateful for the younger girl's brisk, no-nonsense attitude to her work.

In the middle of one of the most frantic afternoons Sister Kenton came hurrying into Labour Ward, where Joanna and Dorothy were tidying up after one delivery, knowing it wouldn't be long before the next.

'Call from Flying Squad, Sister Boyd,' she said briskly.

'They're just leaving for Hanover Park to pick up a patient, and you'll have to go out with them. Sounds like a ruptured uterus, I'm afraid. You know where to go? Good girl, they're waiting for you.'

The small ambulance already had its engine revving as Joanna climbed into the cab beside the driver.

The driver—and Jake O'Connor.

'Oh,' Joanna said, taken aback. 'I didn't realise...'

The big doctor moved to give her a little more room.

'We always try to send a doctor and a sister,' he told her equably. 'I happened to be the only one who could make it.'

They were out of the hospital grounds now, and heading for the busy freeway, the ambulance's siren giving them the right of way.

'You haven't been out to one of the MOUS?' Jake asked, and Joanna shook her head. Midwives' Obstetric Units, she reminded herself, were where the women in the township had their babies and went home a few hours later. If there were no complications.

'Sister Kenton said it sounds like a ruptured uterus,' she said, and Jake nodded.

'They're stabilising her, and as soon as we get her in here we'll give her a blood transfusion, a sedative, if she hasn't had one, and get back to the hospital p.d.q.'

One swift glance at their patient confirmed the need for urgent action. She was almost unconscious and deeply in shock, and Jake didn't attempt to examine her as the ambulance raced back towards the hospital.

'The blood transfusion will help to stabilise her,' he said, his voice low, 'and Sister Kenton will see that the theatre is ready for us.'

As he had said, the small labour ward theatre was

ready, and the anaesthetist waiting. Jake examined their patient when she had been moved to the operating table.

'Uterus is a separate mass,' he said quietly. 'Foetal heartbeat?'

'I can't get anything,' Joanna told him. 'But her blood pressure is stabilised now.'

The big doctor's hands were strong and sure on his patient.

'I'm not giving up on this baby,' he said determinedly. 'This tear is too bad for suturing—we'll do a Caesarean and a hysterectomy. Consent form?'

Joanna told him that the sister at Hanover Park had got the form signed, knowing it could be necessary.

After that, there was no time for anything but swift instructions as the doctor made the cut for delivering the baby. No matter how often she saw this done, the swiftness of it always amazed Joanna. She took the baby from the doctor, and handed him to the staff nurse. She herself had to be ready to assist Jake as he performed an emergency hysterectomy. But even in the urgency of this, a cry from the baby stopped them both. For a second his eyes met hers over their masks, and she knew that he was as relieved as she was.

'She'll do now,' he said at last wearily. He turned away from the operating table, and pushed his mask up onto his forehead.

Joanna and her nurse finished cleaning the young woman up and moved her to a trolley. When the staff nurse from the intensive care unit came through, they went over the post-operative care before the trolley was wheeled away.

Joanna went through to the duty room to write up her notes, realising, as she sat down, that she should have been off duty an hour ago. And realising, too, that she was very tired.

'Sister Boyd?'

She looked up, as Jake came in.

'I've just been into the nursery, and the baby is doing fine. A little distressed, obviously, but he's more than holding his own.'

'Thank you, Dr O'Connor,' Joanna said. 'I was just going to look into the nursery myself.'

She put her notes down.

'Coffee?' she asked.

'Shouldn't you be off duty?' he asked.

'I doubt if I'd make it home without coffee first,' she told him, and handed him a mug of steaming coffee. 'You look as if you should be off, too.'

'Ward round first,' he said, 'but this will help me through that. No, I'm not sitting down. If I did, I might never get up again.' He smiled. 'We did a good job, didn't we?'

'We did,' Joanna agreed. 'And at modesty we're tops!'

He laughed, his dark head thrown back.

'You're right,' he said. 'But we did…thanks. It makes all the difference, knowing I can rely on a good sister.'

Thanks to you, too, Dr O'Connor, Joanna thought when he had gone, absurdly pleased at his praise.

Because he's such a good doctor, she reminded herself. That's all.

A day or two later, Joanna had a phone call from Alice just after she got home.

'I got your phone number from Jake,' Alice said.

From Jake? Of course, he would have her housemate David Palmer's number.

'Are you working all day tomorrow, or are you off at

all?' Alice asked. 'The thing is, Philip has to see someone in Claremont, not far from you, and I wondered...that is...' Her voice faltered.

Joanna remembered that Jake had said Alice had always been shy, and after the accident she'd found it even more difficult to reach out to people.

'As it happens, I'm off in the afternoon,' she said. 'Could Philip drop you off here? We could have a cup of tea, sit on the stoep.'

'Would you mind?' Alice's voice was eager. 'Cathy's spending the afternoon with a friend, so I'm free.'

Free? Confined to her wheelchair as she was, she wasn't very free, Joanna thought as she put the receiver down.

But Alice's face was bright and unshadowed when Philip lifted her out of the Land Rover and into that wheelchair the next day. Like a child let out of school, Joanna thought with a rush of affection for this girl she was only beginning to know.

'I'll be back around four,' he said, as he positioned Alice and her chair on the stoep. He forestalled any argument from his wife. 'No, Alice, we can't be any later than that—Cathy will have been at the Seldons long enough. You know how I feel about them. You should have asked me before you said she could go home with Megan.'

Joanna could see that this had been an ongoing discussion before they'd reached her, and as Philip drove off Alice turned to her.

'Sorry about that, Joanna.' She sighed. 'Philip always has been a bit...over-protective about Cathy. He worries about Jane Seldon being casual with the children, but I think it's good for Cathy to have some freedom. Anyway,

I'm enjoying my outing! Let's talk about girls' things, Joanna. I don't often have the chance to.'

Joanna brought out the tray she had ready, and poured tea for both of them. For a while they did talk lightly and easily about girls' things—clothes, hair, make-up. Then Alice asked about Joanna's mother, and her illness, and Joanna told her about that last year and the precious time towards the end.

'It sounds insensitive,' Alice said at last slowly, 'but in a way you were lucky to have that time. My folks were killed in a plane accident, and there was no time to prepare myself, no time to say goodbye.' Her voice was low. 'Cathy was just a baby, she doesn't remember them. Have you a photo of your mother, Joanna?'

Joanna brought out her favourite picture—her mother in the deckchair under the apple tree, Shandy at her feet.

'You're very like her,' Alice said. 'You have the same smile.'

Suddenly, without any conscious decision, Joanna looked directly at her.

'Jake told me there's an operation that could be a possibility for you to walk again, Alice,' she said.

Alice shook her head.

'Jake knows it isn't really a possibility,' she said. 'We couldn't take the risk. You know I have this heart abnormality?'

'Yes, I do know about that,' Joanna said. 'But if you had an angiogram, you could establish whether the operation really would be too risky.'

And then, because even in this short time of knowing this woman somehow she felt close to her, she went on, 'Perhaps you'd rather Jake hadn't said as much as he did, but I know Philip carries this load of guilt about the accident, I know he's afraid of losing you, but...'

Something in Alice's face stopped her.

'You may know that,' she said evenly, 'but there is something no one but Philip and I know. Just before the accident happened we were quarrelling. I said I needed more freedom, I couldn't take him being so possessive. I said—I said things that shouldn't have been said.'

For a moment she was silent.

'I told him,' she said painfully, 'that if things didn't change, I would leave him, and I would take Cathy with me. I—I think he turned to look at me then, and that's why he didn't manage to avoid the tractor.'

Her hands were clasped together in her lap and, as Joanna watched, she turned her wedding ring round slowly.

'So, you see, it was as much my fault as Philip's, and I can't ask anything more of him.'

A slow tide of colour rose in her face as she went on, 'Since then I haven't spoken about it to anyone. I feel as if I'm being disloyal to Philip. But I think maybe I needed to talk about it. You see, Philip and I have never mentioned it again. But I think I knew, even before I knew I wouldn't walk again, that I couldn't leave him.'

Joanna thought about what Philip had said when he'd left Alice.

'But has he changed?' she asked. 'Isn't he still possessive?'

Alice's voice was quiet now, quiet but somehow very sure.

'Yes, he is,' she agreed. 'He hasn't changed, but in many ways I have. He still wants to keep me all to himself, he still resents other claims on me. But through these long months since the accident he has looked after me, he has kept me from anything that might hurt me, he has made a little world where I am safe.'

'And Cathy?' Joanna asked, before she could stop herself.

Alice turned away, but not before Joanna had seen the shadow in her blue eyes.

'Philip will see, as she grows older, that he has to let her go,' she said, but the certainty had gone from her voice.

But only for a moment. Then she lifted her chin, and her eyes were steady.

'What you mustn't forget—what I never forget—is that Philip loves us, Cathy and me, loves us with all his heart.'

Loves you too much, Joanna couldn't help thinking, but there was nothing more she could say, not when Alice's eyes were asking for her understanding.

Impulsively, she stood up and hugged the woman in the wheelchair.

'You're the only one who can make decisions about your life, Alice,' she said. 'But I'm so glad you felt you could talk to me.'

Soon after that, Philip came to take Alice home.

Alice leaned out of the car window as Philip put her wheelchair in the back.

'Joanna, we got talking about so many other things that I forgot what I meant to ask you—will you come to us at Christmas? I know you have Christmas Day and Boxing Day off—I checked with Jake. He's on call on Christmas Eve, then he has the two days off, too. He'll pick you up and bring you through, and you can both stay over—we have plenty of room.'

Christmas, the time she had been dreading, this first Christmas without her mother. But to go to Morgenster, with Jake O'Connor?

'It's very kind of you, Alice,' she said, a little awkwardly. 'I—I'm not sure. Can I let you know?'

Philip came round the car at that moment.

'I thought we were going to have a quiet Christmas, Alice,' he said abruptly.

'And so it will be,' Alice returned. She put her hand on his. 'We've turned down a couple of invitations from folks around us. But it's a family time, Philip, and Jake is your cousin. Just ourselves, and Jake and Joanna.'

Jake and Joanna. Disturbing, the way she had coupled their names, Joanna thought, as she returned Alice's goodbye wave. Very disturbing. She would have to talk about it to Jake.

As it turned out, it was Jake himself who mentioned it first. Joanna had sent for him when she had an undiagnosed breech delivery, and she was glad to have him there because it was a difficult birth, with the cord wound twice around the baby's neck.

'You're doing fine, Mrs Jacobs, just pant and don't push. We'll have this little one out before you know it,' he told their patient.

Joanna had already done an episiotomy to make the delivery easier, and now, expertly, he eased the baby's little bottom out and then the legs.

'There you are,' he said, and the tiny baby gave a good healthy cry. 'She doesn't even need that awkward bottom smacked, does she?'

His bleeper gave an imperious ring, and he hurried off. But when Joanna and Dorothy had delivered the afterbirth, and Joanna had completed the stitching, she found him in the duty room, drinking coffee with Sister Kenton.

'Just a warning,' he said. 'One of my MOU patients is being brought in. The sister out there wanted to make sure I was around.'

Sister Kenton stood up.

'Have some coffee, Sister Boyd,' she said. 'It's my

lunch-hour so I'll go and see what exciting menu we have today! Not that I should be having anything more than a salad,' she said ruefully.

The big Irish doctor smiled.

'Sure and what man could be resisting a cuddly armful like yourself, Sister dear?' he said.

The older woman shook her head.

'You're a terrible man, Dr O'Connor,' she said, and she went out smiling.

Jake, also smiling, put his cup down.

'I hear you had a visit from Alice,' he said.

'Yes, I did,' Joanna replied, annoyed to find herself ill at ease, her cheeks warm. 'She asked me to go to them for Christmas, and she said—'

'She said I would take you there and back? Yes, that's right, if you don't mind missing out on Christmas Eve, I'll pick you up on Christmas morning.'

Then, disarming her completely, he said that perhaps this first Christmas might be less hard for her if she was to do something really different, like that.

'I know that,' Joanna agreed, her voice low. She hesitated, and then, more baldly than she had meant to, she said, 'But I wouldn't want Alice to have the wrong impression about you and me, and I'm sure you wouldn't either.'

He looked down at her, his eyebrows raised, his eyes amused. Joanna, more embarrassed than ever, had no choice but to go on determinedly.

'I think she does have the wrong impression, that's all.'

Jake shook his head.

'Don't worry,' he said cheerfully. 'Alice's ambition in life is to get me paired off. She's been doing it since I came to Cape Town.'

Perhaps he had said it without thinking, Joanna thought,

but she could see that he realised that this was dangerous ground.

He looked down at her, his smile gone. And there was something in the sudden darkness of his eyes, in the tightness of his jaw, that made the breath catch in her throat, made her heart thud unevenly.

'But I don't think that need stop you accepting the invitation for Christmas. After all, you and I understand each other very well, don't we, Sister Boyd?'

And with a cool nod, he turned and left her.

In Labour Ward, the few days before Christmas were much too pressured for Joanna even to notice whether that coolness was still there when she and Jake worked together.

There was another emergency trip to one of the MOUs for Joanna, but this time with David Palmer. And Sister Kenton told her that Dr O'Connor had had to do two unscheduled Caesareans and an emergency hysterectomy, all in one night.

'And he's on call on Christmas Eve,' she said. Which Joanna knew very well because of the coming visit to Alice, but she didn't say anything. Fond as she was already of the older sister, she knew all too well how tongues wagged in hospitals. 'But he has the next two days off, and the poor man is beginning to look as if he needs it.'

The poor man, Joanna couldn't help thinking on Christmas morning, certainly did look as if he could do with a rest. And a shave.

'Sorry about this,' he said, rubbing his hand over his chin. 'Your Mrs Ngala suddenly delivered an hour ago, and since I'd said I'd pick you up at seven and we'd be there for breakfast, I came straight here.'

Joanna had been waiting on the stoep, and he took her small overnight bag from her and put it in his car.

'I have coffee ready,' she said. 'I poured it when I heard your car. You look as if you could do with it.'

He didn't take the mug of steaming coffee from her right away. Instead, he looked down at her for such a long time that she felt a slow tide of colour rising in her cheeks.

'Merry Christmas, Joanna,' he said, and for a ridiculous moment she thought he was going to kiss her. Then, the gentleness of his voice taking her by surprise, he said, 'Did you get through Christmas Eve all right?'

Joanna nodded, her throat suddenly tight. It was so unexpected, this gentleness, from this man, this man she was so sure she had taped. But he meant it—she could see that. She had got through Christmas Eve, but there had been some bad moments, moments when she had been unable to stop herself from remembering last Christmas Eve when she had known, and her mother had known, that it would be the last one.

'It was so different,' she told him, unable to stop herself responding to the very real concern in the dark blue eyes. She had gone with Dorothy and David to the midnight service at the church further along the main road, and they had come back and had the mince pies Rose had left for them before she'd gone off to Kimberley and her Andrew.

'After that I went to bed,' she told Jake. 'I could see that Dorothy and David wanted to be alone. And it was late. I was glad to leave them.'

And I'm glad neither of them are awake now, she thought, for although she'd had to tell Dorothy her Christmas plans, and Jake O'Connor's part in them, she hadn't relished the thought of Dorothy's bright, enquiring eyes putting two and two together and making five, six or even seven.

'Nice dress,' the big Irish doctor said as she got into the car beside him. 'It's a sort of agapanthus colour.'

'I suppose it is,' Joanna agreed, thinking of the tall blue flowers now in bloom. 'I just liked the blue.'

So, she thought, we're going to be pleasant and sociable, and behave in a civilised way. Well, that's fine with me.

The roads out of the city were quiet, and once they were properly in the country she looked towards the distant mountains, which had a blue morning haze on them.

'Everything looks different at this time of day,' she said.

'I love coming out early in summer, before the heat of the day,' Jake said. 'When I'm off duty I sometimes take a Thermos and a sandwich and go off to the beach. I have a long walk and look across Table Bay to the city and the mountain, and then have my coffee and my sandwich. There are never many people around so early.' He glanced at her. 'You'd like that, Joanna.'

'Yes, I would,' Joanna agreed, and it was only as she said it that she wondered if that had been an invitation given and accepted or just a suggestion.

The small town of Stellenbosch was quiet, too, although there were church bells ringing and some people making their way across the green square in the centre of the town. When they drew up outside the Sullivan's house, Cathy and her big golden dog ran down the steps to meet them.

'I've been awake for hours and hours,' she told them, hugging Jake and then quite unselfconsciously lifting her small face up to Joanna to be kissed. 'Would you like to see the things I got in my stocking? We only get proper presents later, but I always get my stocking first,' she explained to Joanna.

'Joanna, Jake, happy Christmas.'

Alice in her wheelchair came round the corner of the stoep. She, too, held out her arms, and Jake and Joanna both bent and kissed her.

'I was going to say we'll have breakfast right away,' she said, laughing, 'but we'll give you five minutes to shave, Jake. You have your usual room, and Joanna is next door.'

There was a long table set round the corner, on the shady side of the big house. By the time Jake came back, his chin smooth and unshadowed, Philip had joined them.

'Just fruit and rolls,' Alice said, as Anna brought out a steaming jug of coffee. 'I thought we'd save ourselves for later.'

It was a casual, happy meal, Joanna thought, and Philip seemed to have forgotten, or set aside, his reservations about sharing Christmas Day with Jake and her. He looked younger, more relaxed, she thought as he took a photo of Cathy giving Simba his present.

'It's a ball,' Cathy said unnecessarily, as she gave the dog the small round parcel. 'He always gets one, but he's always surprised, isn't he, Daddy?'

'He is,' Philip agreed, smiling.

'We just mustn't throw it near the river,' Cathy told them. 'He jumps in even if he knows the ball isn't in the water, and he gets so wet, and Anna gets cross with him 'cos he makes big wet pawmarks all over the house.'

Jake put his cup down, and looked at Philip.

'Do you remember the Christmas we got fishing rods, Philip?' he asked.

'Do I remember? And while the grown-ups were finishing their Christmas dinner, we went off to the river, certain we'd catch the big salmon we'd heard about.'

'And you thought you'd got him, and I tried to help

you, and it was nothing but an old boot!' Jake said, laughing.

'Sure and that wasn't the end of it, though,' Philip told Joanna and Alice. Joanna could see that Alice had also noticed that the two men were both becoming much more Irish as they brought out their boyhood memories. 'For did we not fall in, and we had to make our way home cold and dripping.'

'But we were lucky, for everyone was in such good spirits, as you might say, that they could do nothing but laugh at us,' Jake finished. Both men laughed as they remembered.

And then, as Joanna watched, the laughter left Philip Newton's grey eyes and the guarded distance was back again.

'Time for these presents under the tree now, Cathy,' he said, and he took his small daughter's hand. 'Let's go inside.'

Joanna, looking at Jake, saw the warmth and the smile leave his face, too, and for a moment the bewildered bleakness went to her heart. She had the urge to go to him and put her arms around him, for he looked so much in need of comfort. And then, as she watched, he recovered and followed Alice in her wheelchair, his dark head high, through the wide hall and into the room where Cathy had already shown Joanna the huge Christmas tree.

Perhaps Alice hadn't noticed, Joanna thought, or perhaps she had become expert at smoothing over any difficult moments like that. In any case, she positioned her wheelchair beside the pile of presents at the tree and told her small daughter which ones she could hand out.

Joanna had wondered what to do about presents, and she had eventually decided to get something fairly nominal for everyone. Cathy loved the tiny baby doll in a sleeping bag, and Alice immediately put the blue velvet hairband on her fair curly hair. For each of the two men she had got a new thriller.

'Thanks, Joanna,' Philip said, once again the good and warm host. 'I do enjoy P.D. James. Most folks seem to think a lawyer should be given John Grisham, so it's a nice change.'

Jake thanked her for his Ruth Rendall, and when she admitted that she enjoyed her books as well he promised to lend it to her when he had finished it.

In her turn, Joanna thanked Alice and Philip for the beautiful coffee-table book on Cape Town, and Cathy for the bookmark with rather uneven stitches on it.

'I made it at school,' Cathy told her. 'And when Mummy showed me the book for you, I knew it was just the right thing.'

'It certainly is, Cathy, and I'll always treasure it,' Joanna said, with perfect truth.

'Happy Christmas, Joanna,' Jake said, and he handed her a small parcel. She unwrapped it, and with a gasp of delight took out a silk scarf in soft shades of sea green.

'It's the one I looked at when we walked through the visitors' shop at Kirstenbosch,' she said, and the doctor nodded.

'I went back and got it after you left,' he told her.

And that in spite of…of any hostility between us, Joanna thought, more touched than she would have thought possible.

'Thank you, Jake,' she said again, softly.

'Mummy, Daddy, isn't it my turn now for my special present?' Cathy asked anxiously.

Alice looked at the pile of newly unwrapped Christmas presents beside her daughter, and shook her head.

'Don't you think you've had plenty of presents?' she said.

'Oh, I have, and they're all lovely,' Cathy replied. 'But you and Daddy did say there was a very special present for me, and it wouldn't be under the tree.'

Alice held out her hand to Philip, and he took it.

'Do you think it's time for Cathy's present?' she asked him.

'I think it just might be,' he agreed. 'Oh—here's Anna with coffee. Should we have that first?'

'We'll have it on the back stoep,' Alice said. When they went outside, she said to Anna, 'Stay for a minute, Anna, so that you can see Cathy getting her present.' She turned to the little girl. 'Close your eyes, Cathy, and no peeping.'

Cathy closed her eyes, and Philip went across to a small outhouse. A moment later he came out, leading a sturdy, small, white pony.

'Now you can look,' he said, standing at the steps, the pony's rein in his hands.

Joanna thought she would never forget the look of joy on Cathy's small face as she saw her 'special present'. She ran down the steps, and put her arms around the pony's neck, her face buried against him.

'Can I ride him right now, Daddy?' she asked, and Philip lifted her into the saddle.

'One thing, Cathy,' he said, still holding the reins. 'You are never to ride him unless I'm with you.'

His small daughter looked up at him, her eyes wide.

'But you're not here when I come home from school, Daddy,' she said. 'And sometimes you're not even home when I go to bed.'

'Oh, Philip,' Alice said, 'he's a very gentle pony, and

he's been accustomed to children riding him on their own...'

Anna stepped forward.

'Mr Philip,' she said firmly, 'you can show my Jannie how to look after Cathy on her pony. He will see that she is safe. Cathy, you will do what Jannie tells you.'

'Oh, yes, Anna.' Cathy's small face was earnest. She looked up at her father. After a moment Philip sighed and led the white pony right round the house, Cathy's face alight as she held the reins.

'Push me down the ramp, please, Jake,' Alice said. 'I want to follow them.'

Joanna, about to follow, too, encountered Anna's fierce frown.

'I've looked after Cathy since she was born,' she said, her voice low. 'When she learned to walk, and she fell, I picked her up. But she is not a baby now, she must be allowed to grow up, she must do some things for herself. And her daddy must let her.'

There was nothing Joanna could say to that, and when the procession came back round the corner Anna smiled and clapped her hands in admiration.

'Look at me, Anna. See how well I can ride him. Isn't he lovely, Joanna? I'm going to call him Snowball. Daddy, can he stay here while you have coffee? I want to see him every minute.'

And it was difficult to persuade her, when it was lunch-time, that Snowball couldn't be brought into the dining-room.

It was a cold lunch, beautifully set out—cold turkey, ham, salads and a wonderful fruit salad.

'Took me a while to accept that this is much better in a hot country than a traditional Christmas dinner,' Jake said, as he and Joanna helped themselves from the buffet.

'Yes, I can understand that,' Joanna agreed, her voice low, although the others were back at the table. 'I think it's marvellous, but sometimes it doesn't quite feel as if it's Christmas, in spite of the tree, presents, everything.'

'You'll feel that it's Christmas later,' Jake said mysteriously.

And in the early evening, at dusk, there came the sound in the distance of people singing Christmas carols. Jake pointed to lights coming down the long drive of Morgenster, and then Joanna saw a group of people, some young, some old, men, women, children, carrying lanterns and singing 'Mary's Boy Child'. They reached the stoep, and changed to 'The First Noel'.

'People from the village,' Alice told Joanna softly. 'They do this every Christmas. Isn't it lovely?'

They listened to the singers, and Joanna felt a sting of tears behind her eyes at the simple sincerity of these people.

'Was I right?' Jake murmured, his lips close to her ear. 'Does this not make you feel it really is Christmas?'

'Yes, it does,' Joanna replied, her voice low as well. And for some reason this, more than anything else, brought back last Christmas to her, these same hymns, her mother beside her, thin, tired, but her face bright as she'd joined in the familiar Christmas music. She turned her head away, but not quickly enough for Jake had seen and his arm was around her shoulders for one brief, unbelievably comforting moment.

Then the singing was over, and Anna brought plates of biscuits, sweets and cool drinks for the children, coffee for the adults. When they had finished they went off up the drive again, lanterns swinging, singing 'Still the Night'.

'They're going to the next farm now,' Alice said. She turned to her small daughter. 'Bedtime, Cathy,' she said.

'But, Mummy, some of those children are younger than me,' Cathy protested.

'Maybe, but I bet they weren't awake at five o'clock this morning,' Alice replied. 'I'm sure Anna has your bath run—would you like Joanna to come up with me to say goodnight to you?'

Cathy nodded vigorously.

'And Daddy, too, and Jake,' she said.

When they had all said goodnight to Cathy they came downstairs again, sitting outside and enjoying the slightly cooler night air.

'What's that lovely smell?' Joanna asked. 'I didn't notice it earlier.'

'It's the frangipani,' Philip told her. 'It's exotic, but delicate, isn't it? You smell it more at night.' He pointed out the huge bush at the side of the stoep, and put one of the white, waxy blossoms in her hand. 'There's another bush round the side, just outside your bedroom—you'll smell it there.'

Later, in her pretty rose-sprigged room, Joanna opened the window and sniffed. Yes, he was right, the scent of the frangipani was even stronger here.

She undressed and got into bed, but somehow she wasn't sleepy, in spite of the warm night and the full day with so many new experiences in it. Her silk scarf lay over the back of a white cane chair, and even when she put the light out, the moonlight streaming in the window—for she had left the curtains open for coolness—showed the delicate colours dimly, mistily. Fancy Jake going back to buy it, she thought. He did look tired when we all said goodnight. No wonder, with the night he'd had.

It was a strange and rather a disturbing thought, that he was asleep just through the wall from her. She had a sudden picture of his dark head against the pillow, the lines of his lean brown face relaxed in sleep, the dark lashes—and they were ridiculously long for a man—closed over his blue eyes.

He had looked so hurt in that moment when the closeness between Philip and him had come and gone.

I think I'm in danger of going soft on him, Joanna told herself severely.

She got out of bed, restless and too warm to sleep, with the thought of the swimming pool at the side of the house. Dark and deserted, it would be wonderful to swim right now, all alone. Perhaps if she cooled down she'd be able to sleep.

She put her bikini on, took a towel from the bathroom and tiptoed through to the hall. The big front door would make a noise, she was sure, but there was a door leading out of the small study, she remembered. No sign or sound of Simba, she realised with relief, for a resounding bark or two would have wakened the household.

The water was smooth and silky, and delightfully cooling. She swam a few lengths lazily, then she got out and dived in. Not too good, she thought critically, and she got out to try another dive.

It was as she dived that she remembered Cathy saying seriously that it wasn't a good idea to dive when you were wearing a bikini. And Cathy had been right. In the darkness of the pool she groped for her lost bikini top.

'Good idea, a late night swim,' Jake said conversationally, his voice coming from the darkness at the side of the pool. 'I thought I heard something. I think I'll join you. There's a light somewhere.'

Joanna reached the side of the pool and, in spite of the darkness, stayed well in the protection of the water.

'Don't put the light on,' she said quickly.

'It's great swimming in the dark, isn't it?' Jake said. 'Water nice and warm?'

Joanna took a deep breath.

'Would you mind handing me my towel? It's on the bench.'

'You don't have to cut your swim short because I'm here,' Jake said, laughter in his voice. 'The pool is big enough for both of us.'

'I know that,' Joanna replied. And then, with as much dignity as she could muster, she said, 'It's just that...I seem to have lost my bikini top.'

CHAPTER FIVE

THERE was a moment's silence.

'Well, well,' Jake said thoughtfully, 'and isn't that a problem now?'

'Yes, it is,' Joanna replied. 'So would you, please, pass me my towel?'

'Oh, I can do better than that,' the big doctor said cheerfully. 'If you will just be staying right where you are, with your back modestly to me, I will switch on the light just long enough to locate the missing…garment. Then I will retrieve it for you, and decency will be restored.'

'You're laughing at me,' Joanna accused him.

'Not at you, at your situation,' he replied. 'Right—light going on.' For a moment the pool light went on. It seemed to Joanna quite a long moment, then there was only the moonlight again and a clean splash as Jake dived in. Seconds later, he surfaced beside her.

'Here you are,' he said, and he handed her her bikini top. 'And I shall avert my eyes while you put it on because there isn't a cloud in this night sky and the moonlight is clear and bright. Are you decent now?'

'Yes, I am,' Joanna returned, adding a little stiffly, 'Thanks for getting it for me.'

'And you'll not be accepting a challenge to race, I don't suppose, in case you run into further problems? So we'll just have a gentle swim in this delightfully cool water.'

Joanna had been on the point of getting out before she'd lost her bikini top, but it seemed rather ungracious to do that when Jake had come to the rescue as he had. And it was rather pleasant, she had to admit, swimming together with the moonlight casting a shaft of light on the water. When they did get out, she towelled her hair dry and then wrapped the big towel around herself. Jake's thick, dark hair was even more unruly than usual when he'd finished towelling it.

All at once, now that they were out of the water, Joanna was very conscious of the big dark man so close to her in the warm night.

'Couldn't you sleep either?' she asked quickly, trying to bring some normality to this somewhat strange situation. 'I would have thought you'd be tired, after your busy night.'

'Too tired to sleep, I sometimes find,' he said. 'What I need now is a nice cup of tea. What about we go to the kitchen, and put the kettle on? I know where everything is.'

'I think that's a good idea,' Joanna replied.

But Jake didn't move. In the moonlight, he looked down at her. And then, very gently, he kissed her, his lips surprisingly gentle on hers.

'You know, Sister Boyd,' he said, and his voice was uneven, 'I think we've got to admit, you and I, that something very peculiar happens when we're together.'

Joanna could feel her heart thudding against her ribs, although he hadn't touched her, other than his lips on hers. She tried to match his attempt at lightness.

'You may be right, Dr O'Connor,' she returned. 'I think it's electricity or—or magnetism, or something like that, that's all.'

'Sounds very scientific,' Jake murmured. He touched her lips with his finger, very gently, and then, still gentle, he kissed her again. But his kiss, gentle at first, became more urgent, more demanding, and then his arms were around her, holding her very close to him. I don't think I tried very hard to resist, Joanna thought afterwards, for somehow she found that her arms were around him, and everything in her was responding to the urgency and the demand of his lips on hers, his body against hers.

She had no idea how long it was before they drew apart.

'Strong electricity,' Jake murmured. He took her hand in his. 'Let's have that cup of tea.'

I must be out of my mind, Joanna thought a little later as she and Jake sat at the scrubbed wooden table in the big kitchen, drinking tea, with Simba in his basket near them, so relaxed that he did no more than wag his plumed tail. I don't like this man, I don't trust him, I know far too much about him—so what am I doing here? And why didn't I stop whatever was happening beside the pool?

She wondered afterwards if she should have taken the chance then to talk to him about those things. To say that she couldn't trust him because of the way he had treated Helen Johnson. To tell him even that she knew so well how heartbroken Helen must have been because she had been there herself. But at the same time to say, too, that he'd been right—she had sat in judgement on him. Perhaps even to ask him for his side of the story.

But she didn't do any of these things. Instead, they sat in the kitchen in a strangely companionable silence, and at last, when Jake put his cup down and yawned hugely, Joanna realised that she was sleepy, too.

She rinsed out their cups and set them on the draining-board. They walked along the dark corridor together, and at her door Jake stopped.

'Goodnight, Joanna,' he said, softly, and his lips brushed hers for just a moment. 'See you in the morning.'

'It isn't called Boxing Day here, it's called Day of Goodwill,' Alice explained over breakfast the next day.

'But it's always a holiday.' She glanced out the window at Cathy and her pony, waiting not too patiently for Philip to finish his breakfast and let her ride. And then, warm teasing in her voice, she said, 'Nice swim last night?'

Joanna felt a warm tide of colour flood her cheeks.

'Very nice,' Jake replied equably. 'And a nice cup of tea afterwards. You'd have found the cups, but how did you know about the swim—were we noisy?'

'Not at all, you were very quiet,' Alice said demurely. 'But it was such a hot night we left the curtains open, and I saw the light go on in the pool just for a moment.'

'Oh, yes, of course,' Jake murmured. If you dare mention that I lost my bikini top, Joanna thought, I'll—I'll— Across the breakfast table, she glared at him.

Slowly, carefully, he buttered a piece of toast and hesitated between honey and marmalade.

'We realised we didn't need the light,' he said blandly, taking a spoonful of honey. 'Much nicer, swimming by moonlight, wasn't it, Joanna?'

'Much nicer,' Joanna agreed, relieved.

And the potentially difficult moment was over, although there was a hint of mischief in the big doctor's eyes that made her wonder if he was going to say anything else. But there was no chance, no time, for a moment later Anna came hurrying into the room.

'Dr Jake, you must come quickly,' she said. 'Francie—my Francie, my daughter—the baby was not supposed to come for three weeks, but now she has terrible pains. Come quick.'

Jake turned to Joanna, and there was no need for his quick question and her equally quick reply. She followed him out of the house, when he had grabbed his bag, along the path and into a small whitewashed cottage behind the stables. The girl lying on the bed was very young, and very frightened.

'Well, Francie, I haven't seen you since that time you broke your wrist,' Jake said. 'Let's have a look at you, see if we should be getting you to hospital.'

But Joanna knew, as she watched Jake's swift, professional examination, that there wasn't going to be time.

'Gloves,' he said crisply, and Joanna found two packs of sterile gloves in his bag. He smiled down at the girl on the bed. 'This baby of yours is in a hurry, Francie, but Sister Boyd and I are a good team—we've dealt with quite a few babies together.'

And the next moment there was no doubt that this baby certainly was in a hurry for Francie gave a gasp and the dark little head crowned.

'Easy now,' Jake said. 'Just do what I tell you. Don't push, just pant—you know the way Shandy does, when he's been running round the garden? That's it, good girl. Now—now, Francie, a good push. And another. Hold Sister's hands, and give us one more.'

A moment later he held a small wriggling baby in his hands. Joanna took the baby from him and wrapped the tiny boy in the shawl Anna held out to her.

'And not a stitch needed,' Jake said a little later when Joanna, with the proud grandmother's help, had cleaned Francie up and given her her baby to hold. 'Didn't I say we were a good team, Francie?'

Suddenly shy, the girl buried her face in her baby's shawl, murmuring something.

'She say she will call this baby Goodwill Jake,' her mother said. 'Goodwill for the day and Jake for you, Dr Jake.'

'Oh, thank you, Francie, I'm honoured,' Jake said, and

Joanna thought that this was possibly the first time she had seen him somewhat at a loss.

As they walked back to the house he looked down at her.

'I was right, wasn't I?' he said conversationally. 'We are a good team.'

Now it was Joanna's turn to be at a loss, and she said nothing in reply. Because, of course, he was right—they were a good team. But there was something very disturbing in his eyes that seemed to say a great deal more than the simple words.

Amazingly, after all the excitement, it was a pleasant, relaxed day, and in the evening, when Joanna and Jake were getting into the car, Philip said to Joanna quietly that he was glad she had come.

'Alice enjoys being with you, I can see that,' he said. He went on, with difficulty, 'I like seeing her laugh, and you do make her laugh. She...used to laugh so much more when I knew her first.'

She hasn't got a great deal to laugh about, Joanna thought soberly, looking at Alice in her wheelchair, helping little Cathy to try on the blue Alice band.

'You will come again soon, won't you, Joanna?' Alice asked anxiously, when Jake and Joanna were in the car. 'You don't have to wait for Jake to have time off. You could come on your own now that you have a car.'

'You have to come soon, Joanna,' Cathy told her imperiously, 'so that you can see how good I'm going to be on Snowball.'

'I will come, Cathy,' Joanna promised. 'Thanks again, Alice, Philip, it's been a marvellous Christmas.'

Marvellous and...strange, disturbing, she thought as she turned for a last wave at the bend of the drive. Would Jake make any reference to last night, she wondered as they drove through the small town and out onto the freeway.

To her relief, he didn't. Instead, he talked about their work in the hospital and asked her if she was happy on Maternity Block.

'I love it,' Joanna replied. 'I do sometimes think I should get myself some more experience—maybe work in Theatre for a while. But I do love being a midwife, and I'm only too happy to be like Sister Kenton and stick with my mothers and babies.'

Jake smiled.

'I'd have to agree,' he said. 'Years ago, when Prof Symms suggested I should specialise in obstetrics, it was too good a chance to miss so I took it. Now I can't see myself in any other field. And, of course, at Groote Schuur we get everything interesting coming our way. The infertility clinic, for one, has made terrific progress. I'd like to see it develop to a stage where we can cut down on multiple births—they're always risky. Just last week we did a scan on a patient—you can look forward to triplets in five months.'

'I've delivered twins,' Joanna said, 'but no more. How long will you let her go?'

'We'll probably bring her into hospital around thirty weeks, and then monitor her condition. I doubt if she'll go much beyond thirty-eight weeks,' Jake told her. 'Then, of course, we'll do a Caesarean. So far the babies are coming on nicely. They'll be tiny, but you know how efficient our neonatal unit is—they can cope.'

'I'm sure they can,' Joanna agreed. 'It's how the poor parents cope when they get the babies home that I wonder about. One baby, even two, that's manageable, but three or more!'

'Yes, I certainly prefer them one at a time,' Jake said.

So many times, Joanna thought, she had seen this man holding a newborn baby, and had seen the relief and the warmth on his face at another safe delivery, another new life. Now, sitting here with him in the car, in a small world that somehow seemed far from the hospital and the professional life they shared, she found herself wondering how he would look holding a child of his own.

It was a strangely disturbing thought, and she wondered why it had come into her head.

'You're on call tonight, aren't you?' she said quickly.

He glanced at her, amusement in his eyes because they had talked about him being on call at the start of their arrangements, and she could see that he was conscious of her sudden awkwardness. Although fortunately not, she told herself, of what had caused it.

'Yes, I am, that's why we had to come away now. And you're on duty at seven tomorrow.'

The old house was silent as he drew up beside it, and Joanna was glad of that. She asked Jake if he wanted to come in for coffee, but he said he didn't have time, and she was glad of that, too. He lifted her overnight bag from the boot and put it down on the step as she unlocked the door.

'Thank you for taking me to Morgenster, Jake,' Joanna said. And in case he felt she was presuming too much, she held out her hand.

He took it in both of his. His eyes were very dark as he looked down at her, and she thought he was going to say something more than a brief goodbye. For a moment, the very air seemed to charged with a tension that made Joanna's heart thud unevenly. Then Jake seemed to change his mind, and he released her hand. But as he drove off he raised one hand and waved.

'Did you have a marvellous time?' Dorothy asked eagerly, when she came home a little later, just off duty.

'Yes, it was lovely,' Joanna replied sedately, but with complete truth.

Dorothy sighed.

'I can't believe you've spent two days with Jake O'Connor, and that's all you can say,' she said accusingly. 'Are you seeing him again?'

'Oh, yes,' Joanna told her. As Dorothy leaned forward eagerly, she went on, laughing, 'Tomorrow morning, for sure, when he does his ward round.'

The younger girl shook her head.

'You know very well that isn't what I meant, but I can see I'm not going to get anything more out of you!'

That's because I don't know, Joanna thought later in her room. I don't know whether Jake will want us to meet again—and I don't know if I want that.

As they had all expected, the next few days were pretty frantic, with babies arriving earlier than expected and unbooked pregnancies with complications being sent to the hospital from the various MOUs.

But sometimes, after a difficult delivery, when mother and baby were both safe, Joanna would find Jake's eyes meeting hers for a brief, shared moment. A moment that gave her a ridiculously warm feeling in the region of her heart, she had to admit.

Having had Christmas off, both she and Jake were on duty over New Year, but although they were rushed off their feet on the last day of the year everything seemed to quieten down around midnight, so that Jake, Joanna, Dorothy and a student nurse were sitting in the duty room as the bells rang out to bring in the New Year.

'Happy New Year,' Jake said, and solemnly raised his

cup of coffee. Then, deliberately Irish, he looked around the small group. 'Sure and I wish for all of you all that you would wish for yourselves.'

He stood up.

'I'm thinking that this is an occasion when we can be forgetting such things as rules and regulations,' he said.

He kissed the student nurse, causing a flood of colour on her dusky skin, and then he kissed Dorothy, with the same reaction.

'Happy New Year, Sister Boyd,' he said, and he kissed Joanna, his lips warm on hers. It was a kiss no different from the kiss he had given the other two, but for a moment his eyes met hers and she knew with complete certainty that he, too, was thinking of their kiss beside the swimming pool in the moonlight.

'And now I think I'd better see how they're doing along in the neonatal unit,' he said, and at the door he turned and blew a kiss to all of them.

'He's an absolute honey,' Dorothy said fervently.

'What about David?' Joanna teased her. 'Isn't he a honey, too?'

The younger girl smiled.

'David's for real,' she said softly. 'Jake O'Connor is for dreams. For me, anyway.'

David's for real. It was a nice way she had put it, Joanna thought. And she preferred not to take the thought any further, as far as she herself was concerned.

A few nights later, she got home to find a note from Dorothy to say that she and David had gone to a party, and she had left directions in case Joanna wanted to join them. But Joanna was only too glad to look forward to a peaceful night on her own. She ran a bath, and while it was running tied her hair back and washed her face. Just as she was about to get into the bath the doorbell rang.

Rose, due back from Kimberley, had forgotten her key, she thought as she ran barefoot through the hall and opened the door.

Jake stood there.

'I should have phoned,' he said, 'but I just took a chance.' He frowned. 'There's water running.'

'My bath!'

When she came back he looked down at her, and she was all too conscious of her scrubbed face and her hair tied back. Not to mention the towel wrapped around her.

'You were getting ready to have an early night?' he asked, and suddenly the awkwardness was gone for that was all too obvious. Joanna burst out laughing, and so did Jake.

'It's a beautiful night, and the mountain is still floodlit. I wondered if you'd like to have something to eat, and then we could drive up Signal Hill and look at the lights of the city. It's something everyone should do in Cape Town.'

Taken aback, Joanna's thoughts whirled.

'Do you think that's a good idea?' she said doubtfully. And she saw, by the momentary stillness of his face, that he knew she had meant much more than his suggestion.

'I think it's a very good idea,' he replied. 'There are things we should talk about, Joanna.'

He looked down at her.

'I keep seeing you wrapped in a towel,' he said, and now there was laughter in his voice. 'Put some clothes on, and we'll go and find somewhere to eat. I have a bottle of wine in the car.'

'And we have fresh rolls. Dorothy left a note to tell me that,' Joanna said. 'How about if I fill a couple, and we make do with that?'

He sat in the kitchen with her while she put ham and

cheese and tomato on the rolls. She looked up, once, to find him looking at her, his eyes very dark with something extremely disturbing in them. So disturbing that she stopped, the knife in her hand.

'Are you going to stab me with that?' Jake asked, and he smiled.

She shook her head.

'No, I—I was just going to ask you if you liked mustard,' she said.

A little later, as they drove up Signal Hill, Joanna looked at Table Mountain, floodlit for summer, a little eerie but breathtaking. And then, from as far up Signal Hill as they could drive, they could see the lights of Cape Town spread out below them.

'I had no idea it would be so beautiful,' Joanna murmured, as Jake opened her window.

'Yes, it is,' he agreed, and his voice was low, too. 'Seeing the lights from Signal Hill is one of the traditions of Cape Town.'

He put his arm around her, and with one hand on her chin he turned her face towards his.

'And this,' he said, not quite steadily, 'is another tradition when you come up Signal Hill at night.'

His lips were warm on hers, and his kiss was gentle. After a moment he drew back.

'I am trying very hard to see that we take things slowly, you and I,' he said. 'And it isn't easy. We do have to talk, we have to clear the air, but for now let's have our picnic.'

He took a rug from the car, and they sat on the grass, ate their rolls and drank some wine.

'I'm not too good at directions,' Joanna said. 'Where is the hospital from here?'

They stood up, and walked over to the small stone wall. Jake pointed out the hospital, and then, almost below them, the Waterfront, with Sea Point beyond it.

'And there are ships out in the bay—look,' he said, pointing to the distant lights.

He poured another glass of wine when they sat down again. For a long time he was silent, and Joanna waited. He was right. They did have to talk—they had to clear the air between them before there was any chance of going on from here.

She admitted to herself that it was what she wanted, in spite of all her fear, all her mistrust of this man, in spite of everything she had been so sure she knew about him.

Afterwards, she wondered many times if things would have been different if they had been able to talk that night, as Jake intended. But from the car there came the shrill, imperious ring of his mobile.

'Damn,' he said forcibly. 'I'm not on call.'

But he stood up, and walked back to the car. A few moments later he came back to her.

'Prof Symms has had a heart attack,' he told her. 'There's an emergency Caesarean, and there's no one else available. I'm sorry, Joanna.'

'I'm sorry, too, Jake,' Joanna said, meaning it with all her heart. She took his outstretched hand and stood up, and with an effort she smiled. 'But that's life. Let's go.'

The phone call, and Jake's boss's heart attack, meant even more pressure on Jake than usual. Joanna understood that very well, and she and the rest of the staff did all they could to lighten his workload and not call on him unless it was absolutely necessary.

And she understood, too, what Jake was saying, in a

few snatched moments after a difficult birth, when she made coffee for him in the duty room.

'I think she'll be all right now,' he said, frowning, 'but let me know if her blood pressure rises again. She should be stable, but with toxaemia you can't be certain. Although he's small, that baby is a fighter—you can always tell, can't you?'

'Yes, you can,' Joanna agreed, and she thought of the tiny baby, now in the ICU, with tubes attached to his frail body, a body that hadn't been ready to face the world for another few weeks. But, yes, he was a fighter.

Jake drained his cup, and set it down.

'That saved my life. Now I can go back to the gynae ward and check my ladies there.' At the door he turned.

'I'm sorry about the other night,' he said. 'And I'm afraid it might be some time before I have much in the way of a free evening.'

'It's all right,' Joanna replied, meaning it. 'There's plenty of time.'

Time to talk, time to clear the air, as he had obviously intended that night on Signal Hill. And after that—time for what?

Time to take it from there, she told herself firmly.

It was a day or two later that she woke up in the morning with her head aching and her limbs like lead. Shouldn't have stayed up so late, watching that Academy Award programme, she told herself. Snap out of it, Joanna!

But a shower and hot, strong coffee with her toast didn't help as much as she'd hoped, and in the middle of the morning Sister Kenton, coming in from a meeting, looked at her sharply.

'You shouldn't be here, Sister Boyd,' she said severely. 'There's all this Sydney flu about, and I am not having my mothers and babies exposed to it! Go and see the staff doctor, and then go home and go to bed.' Then, her voice softening, she said, 'Anyway, my dear, you look dreadful. You should never have come to work today.'

Joanna finished the charts she was working on, and then dragged herself off to the staff doctor. She waited in a long queue of nurses and other staff who all looked as miserable as she felt, and finally, when she had been given her sick certificate and some pills, she made her way down the hill from the hospital to the house, very glad that she hadn't brought her car. The way she felt, driving wouldn't have been a very good idea.

The old house was cool and quiet for Rose, Dorothy and David were all working, and she was glad of that. She took two of the pills she had been given and collapsed into bed, feeling too ill even to make herself a cup of tea. By the time Dorothy, and then Rose, came off duty she felt, if anything, even worse.

'You look awful,' Dorothy told her, 'and you've got a raging temp. I'll bring you some tea. Want anything to eat?'

Even shaking her head hurt, Joanna found.

She drank some tea obediently, and then fell into an uneasy sleep, full of violent dreams that made her wake suddenly, her heart thudding. She had just come back from the bathroom and was looking in the mirror, realising that she looked as bad as she felt, when the door opened.

'I'm sorry, Joanna,' Dorothy said, obviously flustered, 'but he insists on seeing you.' Then, in a whisper, she said, 'I knew you wouldn't want him to see you looking so awful, but he won't listen.'

The next moment Jake was there, crossing the room and taking her hands in his.

'Sister Kenton was right to send you home,' he said quite brusquely. 'You shouldn't be out of bed at all.'

'I had to go to the bathroom,' Joanna protested.

'You can't possibly stay here on your own,' he told her. 'You need looking after, and the other girls are away most of the time. Now, this is what I think...'

Dorothy had gone, ostentatiously leaving the door open. Joanna tried to concentrate on what Jake was saying, but her head was throbbing, and the room seemed to be whirling.

'I'm sorry,' she managed to say, 'I—I'll have to lie down, Jake.'

And then the floor was coming up to meet her in a most unpleasant way, and she was only just conscious of Jake catching her as she fell. She didn't want him to go away. She wanted him to stay there with her, but there wasn't time to say that as darkness engulfed her.

She didn't know how much later it was when she opened her eyes. Her head still felt dreadful, but the room had stopped whirling. She remembered Jake being there, and she remembered that he had been saying something but she hadn't been able to take it in. When I feel better, she thought, I'll thank him for coming to see me.

Carefully, she turned her head, grateful that although it still throbbed the dizziness had gone.

And there, in the chair beside the bed, was Jake, asleep.

Unshaven, obviously exhausted.

He opened his eyes.

'What are you doing here?' Joanna asked him, bewildered.

'You said don't go away,' he said simply. 'So I stayed.'

So I did say it, I didn't just think it, she realised, embarrassed and dismayed.

'You shouldn't have,' she murmured. 'When you're so busy at the hospital.'

He patted his mobile.

'Quieter day for once,' he told her. 'And if I'd been needed, I would have been called.'

She tried to sit up, but realised it wasn't a good idea, for the dizziness returned in full force.

'Lie down,' Jake told her authoritatively.

She lay down.

'How do you feel?' he asked her.

'Better than I did before,' she said, adding, with honesty, 'But not too good.'

He smiled, and something about his smile, in that weary and unshaven face, made her heart turn over.

'You certainly don't look very good,' he told her. 'In fact, you look pretty awful.' His hand on her forehead was cool. 'You're not as fevered as you were but, really, you shouldn't be alone here.'

Yes, that was what he had been saying, she remembered now. She tried to shake her head, but found that it still wasn't a good idea.

'Nonsense,' she said, as firmly as she could. 'It's only flu. I'll be fine.'

'I'll think of something,' Jake returned, equally firmly. He looked at his watch. 'I have to get back to the hospital. And I must shave before my patients see me.'

'Never mind your patients,' Joanna said. 'What about Sister Kenton?'

'Yes, indeed,' Jake agreed. For a moment he put his hand against her cheek, and there was something so unexpectedly tender about his touch that her breath caught in her throat. She knew, shaken and bewildered, that she had never in her life felt like this. In the years since Cliff, she had tried to believe, tried to persuade herself, that she wouldn't ever again be so blind, so trusting, so open to hurt. But she hadn't thought that any man could have made her feel like this. Especially a man like Jake O'Connor.

She heard him talking to Dorothy as he left, and then the sound of his car as he drove off. Dorothy came through, in uniform, a cup of coffee in one hand and a slice of toast in the other.

'I'm glad I came home for that couple of hours I had off,' she said, 'otherwise our Jake might have stood outside, waiting for someone to hear him.' Then, her dark curly head on one side, she said thoughtfully, 'Mind you, I get the impression he would have broken the door down if necessary. Sorry, Joanna, you're not feeling well enough to be teased. I'll bring you some tea and toast. Rose says she'll try to look in later. Will you be all right?'

'I'll be fine,' Joanna assured her. 'Never mind the toast, though—a cup of tea will be heaven.'

A cup of tea and a good sleep, she thought. Dorothy stood over her as she took her next lot of pills, and before Joanna had finished drinking her tea she felt her eyelids grow heavy, and she was barely conscious of Dorothy looking in to say she was going before Joanna was asleep.

She woke much later, with the sun shining in even through the sunfilter curtains. Cautiously, she moved her head and found that, although she felt light-headed, the dizziness seemed to have gone. She reached for her dressing-gown so that she could go and make tea for herself. Ridiculous, she thought as she stood up, that her legs should feel like cotton wool in this short time. But people who had had this Sydney flu did say it hit very hard.

In the kitchen, she switched the kettle on, and suddenly had to sit down while she waited for it to boil. She had just made her tea when the front doorbell rang. Whoever it is, they'll go away, she told herself, but the bell rang again. Then she heard her name being called. Not Jake, not David, so who could it be?

To her astonishment, Philip Sullivan stood at the door.

'I've been sent to take you home to be looked after properly,' he said, a little awkwardly. 'Alice had an SOS from Jake.' He looked at her. 'You certainly look as if you could do with some looking after,' he said. 'Alice says don't even bother bringing anything—she'll lend you whatever you need.'

Ridiculously, Joanna felt her eyes fill with tears.

'It really isn't necessary, Philip,' she said, unable to keep her voice steady. 'It's only flu, and I wouldn't want to take any germs to Alice or Cathy. Or you.'

Philip took her arm, and walked her back to the kitchen and a welcome chair.

'Anna will look after you,' he told her, 'until your flu germs have gone. Jake says you're booked off for at least a week, and he says you're not to argue.'

He smiled, and for the first time Joanna saw that there was a fleeting likeness between the cousins.

'I daren't go back without you,' he said. 'Alice will never forgive me if I do.'

It was easier to give in than to resist, and there was something very appealing about the thought of being looked after. Joanna did put a few necessary things into a small suitcase, and wrote a note to tell her housemates where she had gone.

Philip put her in the back of his Range Rover, lying on the comfortable seat, a pillow under her head, in spite of her protests. She closed her eyes because her head ached less that way, and the next thing she knew they had arrived at the big house.

Alice was on the stoep, in her wheelchair, with Cathy beside her.

'I'm not risking passing on germs,' Joanna told Philip, and he went out and spoke to his wife and his small daughter. With obvious reluctance, they went inside, and a moment later Anna came out.

'You just lean on me, Miss Joanna,' she said comfortably. 'I've got a bed ready for you, and a hot lemon drink, and when you've had that, I'll cool you down with a nice sponging, and then you can sleep.'

And that was just what happened. Afterwards, Joanna found that she didn't remember a great deal about the next two days. There were blurred impressions of Anna beside her bed, giving her a hot and sweet lemon drink, sponging her so that she felt cool and comfortable. Once she heard Cathy's voice quite close, and a loud bark from Simba, but soon there was silence again.

Then at last she woke to find that her head was miraculously clear, and she felt cool without needing to be sponged. Cautiously, she moved her legs, and found that much of the heavy aching had gone.

'You're getting better now,' Anna said with satisfaction, coming in with a tray with a plate of something hot. 'Now, you eat, and get really better quickly. Chicken soup.'

Chicken soup, in the middle of summer? But Joanna found, to her surprise, that nothing could have been more right.

'That was delicious, Anna,' she said, as she finished. 'I haven't had chicken soup brought to me in bed since…since…' Her voice faltered. It was when she'd had her appendix out, in her second year as a student nurse, and she had gone home to convalesce. Chicken soup, brought to her by her mother.

She turned away, but not quickly enough.

'Chicken soup like your mother make?' Anna said gently. 'Miss Alice told me your mother died last year.' She shook her head. 'It doesn't matter how old you are, the hurt when your mother die. Miss Alice said that.'

She poured tea now, and held out the cup to Joanna.

'You've known Alice a long time?' she asked.

'I look after her from when she was a baby,' Anna said. 'Then I look after Cathy.' Her dark eyes clouded. 'When Cathy began to grow up, I think maybe soon we have another baby for me, but then this accident. And now Cathy is not a baby any longer, but her father still treat her like one, and that is not good, it worry Miss Alice, it make her unhappy.'

She stood up, her lips compressed. As if, Joanna thought, she had said enough, or perhaps too much.

'Tomorrow Miss Alice can come to see you,' she said. 'No more flu germs, I think. Or maybe you feel well enough to sit outside. Fresh air and sunshine is good, too.'

The next day, after she had had some fruit and toast for breakfast, Joanna dressed in the blue cotton dress she had hastily put into her small case and made her way through the big cool rooms to the stoep, where Anna had said Alice was.

'Joanna—I'm so glad to see you. Anna can be an absolute dragon sometimes!' Her face alight, Alice held out both hands to Joanna. 'How do you feel?'

'Surprisingly wobbly,' Joanna told her truthfully. 'Alice, I don't know how to thank you for this, sending Philip for me, having Anna look after me.'

There was mischief in Alice's blue eyes.

'I got this phone call from Jake,' she said demurely, 'telling me in no uncertain terms that somehow we were to arrange to look after you. Oh, that reminds me—he's phoned a few times to ask how you were, and he said last night that he'll try to come through tomorrow. Apparently they've managed to get help from one of the private clinics, so he isn't quite as pushed.'

She looked at her watch.

'I have my weekly session with my physiotherapist,' she said. 'She comes out from Stellenbosch, and she gives me some treatment, and we have a session in the pool. Sit quietly here—there are some magazines over there, and Anna will bring you coffee. But I'm warning you, she'll chase you back to bed to have a rest pretty soon.'

'I don't think I would like to argue with Anna,' Joanna said, with perfect truth. And when Anna did come and tell her it was time for a rest, she found that she was only too glad to lie down and close her eyes.

In the afternoon, when Philip brought Cathy home from school, the little girl wanted Joanna to see how good she was on her pony.

'I'm sorry, sweetheart, but I have to get right back to the office,' her father said. 'Maybe tonight.'

Cathy's blue eyes filled with tears.

'But I want to show Joanna now,' she insisted. 'Jannie has been with us every time, Daddy, he can look after me.'

'Philip,' Alice said very quietly, and Joanna could see that this had been discussed before. Philip's mouth tightened.

'All right,' he said, his voice low. 'I'll just have a word with Jannie.'

Five minutes later, he came back with Anna's grandson, Jannie. Philip himself lifted Cathy up onto her pony, and handed the leading rein to the young man.

'Remember, Jannie, she's just to walk, no trotting,' he said.

Joanna thought young Jannie looked after Cathy very responsibly, and she said so to Alice.

Alice sighed.

'I knew he would,' she said. 'But Philip doesn't find it easy to let go.'

Of you as well as of Cathy, Joanna thought the unsaid words would have been. But it wasn't something that could be talked about easily, especially now, with Cathy's small face vivid with joy as she rode past them for the fourth time.

'You're very good, Cathy,' she said.

'Yes, I am,' the child agreed, and Joanna's eyes met Alice's in shared and suppressed laughter. 'We could show Daddy tonight, couldn't we, Mummy? Then he won't worry so much.'

This time there was no laughter in the way Alice's eyes met hers, Joanna thought.

The next morning, very casually, she asked Alice if Jake would be coming. Yes, he had been pretty certain, Alice told her, but he didn't know when. There was a warm questioning in her blue eyes, but Joanna rose hastily from the breakfast table and said she thought she'd wash her hair.

Later, when Alice was in the kitchen with Anna, Joanna took the big shady hat Alice had lent her and went out into the garden. There was a small orchard beyond the pool, with apricots, apples, pears, plums, guavas and litchis growing. And I'm getting to know them all, she thought, peeling the hard skin from a litchi. Then, because it was her favourite, she took an apricot, warm from the sun, and ate it.

'Not quite the Garden of Eden,' Jake said, appearing beside her. 'And not quite forbidden fruit.'

He looked down at her.

'You look a lot better than you did last time I saw you.'

Joanna coloured, remembering all too well that moment of waking to find Jake asleep at the side of her bed because she had asked him to stay with her.

'Thank you for—for arranging all this,' she said awkwardly. 'It's been very nice, being looked after.'

Jake shrugged.

'I knew Alice would be very angry if she heard I'd left you there, so ill. And I gather you wouldn't have her near you until you felt it was safe.'

'Anna insisted that she wouldn't catch any of my germs once I didn't have a temperature,' Joanna told him, and she smiled. 'Anyway, a couple of days more, and I'll be back at work. I could go back through with you today.'

He shook his head.

'It will do you more good to stay on here,' he said.

They had reached the last row of trees, and the green lawn opened up ahead of them. Jake stopped, and took both her hands in his.

'You do look so much better,' he said.

'You said that before,' Joanna reminded him, all at once a little breathless.

'So I did.'

He kissed her, his lips gentle on hers. And then less gentle, his own urgency awaking a response in Joanna that made her forget everything but this man, holding her so close to him.

'Electricity? Or was it magnetism?' Jake murmured at last, his lips still close to hers. 'I've always had this strong belief in scientific experiments.'

'You're laughing at me,' Joanna accused him, not quite steadily.

'Do you mind?' he asked her.

Wordless, she shook her head.

He took her hand in his as they walked out of the orchard into the bright sunshine. A golden day, Joanna thought, dazed and dazzled. A golden day.

She had no premonition of the dark clouds that were to change her golden day completely.

CHAPTER SIX

IT WAS indeed a golden day—a day to remember, Joanna thought, then and later. What was it her mother used to say of a day like that? A day of small things.

The three of them, Jake, Joanna and Alice, sitting on the stoep having coffee, while Jake talked of boyhood memories of Philip and himself, growing up in Ireland. A swim before lunch, both Jake and herself, she knew very well, remembering that moonlight swim. Fruit and cheese and fresh brown bread on the cool, shady side of the stoep, the grapes newly picked. Jake insisting that she was to rest after lunch, and agreeing that lying down on the couch outside would do. The murmur of his voice, and Alice's, as she lay half asleep, half awake in the warmth of the afternoon. Cathy, brought home from school by a neighbour, her small face alight when she saw Jake. The big golden dog solemnly giving Jake a paw when he left in the late afternoon.

And a fleeting goodbye kiss, Jake's lips warm on Joanna's cheek as he promised to come and pick her up in two days to take her back to Cape Town.

Afterwards, she remembered thinking as he drove off with a final wave that they still had to have that talk, she and Jake. Somehow, right then, clearing the air between them didn't seem to have the importance she had placed on it before. We're doing quite nicely without that, she thought. Then, smiling at her own philosophical turn of mind, Perhaps yesterday is less important than today and tomorrow.

Philip didn't come home until after dinner—he'd had to take a client out, Alice told Joanna. Cathy was already in bed, but he went up to say goodnight to her. Alice and Joanna, discussing the film they had watched on TV the night before, both stopped when he came in, for it was all too clear that something was wrong.

'So Jake was here today,' he said abruptly.

'Yes, he was sorry to miss you, but he had to get back,' Alice replied. Determinedly bright, she went on, 'But he's coming back in a couple of days to take Joanna back to Cape Town. You'll probably see him then.'

'Of course, to take Joanna back,' Philip said levelly.

I think I should get out of here, Joanna thought. It's becoming extremely awkward. But before she could say anything Alice turned her wheelchair and headed out of the room. At the door she said, over her shoulder, the determined brightness now a little shaky, 'I think I'll have an early night. I'll just get Anna to help me bath. See you in the morning, Joanna.'

For a moment Joanna thought Philip was going to go after her, then he turned back. Joanna's resentment and anger faded as she saw the unhappiness on his face.

'I'm—sorry, Joanna,' he said, with difficulty. He tried to smile. 'Nothing to do with you.'

I could just leave it there, Joanna thought, and walk away. But there was the memory of Jake's face, troubled and distressed, when he'd told her that for some reason he and Philip had lost their boyhood closeness. And there had been that brittle brightness in Alice's voice a moment ago.

She took a deep breath.

'Jake was telling us today about the time the two of you were playing in the old rowing boat at the lough, and the boat floated away, and Jake's father had to wade in, fully dressed, to pull you back. You remember that, too?'

Philip nodded.

'Yes,' he said, very quietly. 'I remember.'

Joanna leaned forward.

'What went wrong between you and Jake, Philip?' she asked gently. 'I know it makes him unhappy.'

Philip lifted his head, and now there was a cool hostility in his grey eyes.

'Makes him unhappy, does it?' he said, and his voice was harsh. 'Well, he shouldn't have to look too far to find the reason.'

'He doesn't know why,' Joanna told him steadily. 'Look, Philip, are you not taking out some of your own unhappiness and guilt on Jake?'

'Guilt?' he shot back.

I'm right in this now, Joanna thought. I have to go on.

'Yes, guilt,' she repeated. 'Guilt because of the accident, because Alice is in a wheelchair.'

He was silent for so long, his face tight, controlled, that she began to wish she hadn't said anything.

'What do you know about the accident, Joanna?' he asked, very carefully.

'Perhaps more than you would want me to,' Joanna replied. 'Alice told me that—that just before it happened she told you that she was thinking of leaving you.'

'And did she tell you why?' Alice's husband asked.

Joanna lifted her head and looked straight at him.

'Because you were too possessive. You wouldn't give her enough freedom.' Then, a little afraid of the still anger in his face, she said, 'She told me that she said things she shouldn't have, that she...'

Something in Philip's face stopped her.

'She didn't tell you what those things were,' he said flatly.

Joanna shook her head, and now she wished with all her heart that she hadn't got into this.

'She told me she was in love with someone else, that that was why she was thinking of leaving me. As well as because of my other faults.'

She waited, a deep and dark misery creeping through her whole body as she began to realise what Philip was telling her.

'It was Jake, of course,' Philip said. 'There were a few things I'd been wondering about—it all came together. She didn't have to say his name.' His eyes were shadowed, remembering. 'There wasn't time then because that was when the tractor turned in front of us. And afterwards...she didn't want to talk about it, she asked me to forget all that she had said. I've tried, by heaven I've tried, but I can't.'

Joanna stood up.

'No, I don't suppose you can,' she said, and she could hear her own voice as if it belonged to someone else. Cool, steady. Reasonable.

Philip stood up, too.

'I don't know why I've told you all this,' he said, abrupt again. 'I haven't told anyone since it happened. Alice has never mentioned it from the day of the accident. The only thing she said, and that was before she knew she wouldn't walk again, was that she wanted me to forget all that she had said.'

And, of course, Joanna thought with complete clarity, once you knew you had a wife who was in a wheelchair, you knew, too, that you weren't going to lose her, that she was yours, yours to care for, to protect, for always.

'Goodnight, Philip,' she said quietly.

It was a long night, a black night, in every way. It seemed right somehow that there was no moonlight, that there were clouds hiding the stars as Joanna sat at her open window, or lay wide awake on her bed.

Such a short while ago she had smiled at herself when she'd thought that yesterday didn't matter, that it was today and tomorrow that were relevant and important. 'I was wrong,' she said aloud, in the silence of her bedroom. 'I was so wrong.'

Because yesterday did matter. Yesterday, and what Jake had done in betraying his cousin's trust, in taking advantage of Alice's unhappiness—that was unforgivable.

In a strange way she didn't feel that Alice was to blame. She could see that Philip's possessiveness, his inability to give Alice any space, any freedom, had made her all too vulnerable, all too open to Jake's warmth and charm.

Oh, yes, Joanna thought with bitterness. It wouldn't have been difficult for Jake to make Alice fall for him, feeling the way she did.

She could see now, all too clearly, that she should never have changed her mind about him. Her initial distrust, because of the way he had treated Helen Johnson, had been so right. Why had she ever allowed herself to feel differently towards him?

Alone in the darkness, her cheeks burned with shame when she remembered his arms around her, his lips on hers, and her body's immediate response to his. He must have thought I was easy game, she thought bitterly. Like everyone else. He must have laughed at me, with my talk of electricity, of magnetism, with my poor attempts to hold out against him.

She didn't cry. The heaviness of her heart was beyond tears, but when at last she fell asleep she dreamed that she was crying. A strange, disturbed dream of being a child again, of a doll she had lost in the garden of the cottage. In her dream, she was searching for her lost doll, looking under bushes, behind a garden seat. And going to her mother, weeping, because she couldn't find the doll she had lost.

But when she woke her eyes were dry, although her throat was tight.

'You don't look nearly as well as you did yesterday, Joanna,' Alice said, concerned. 'Maybe you overdid things, swimming and walking with Jake.'

'I'm all right, really,' Joanna replied. 'I just didn't sleep too well. I think I must be needing to get back to work.'

Having said that, there was the realisation that Jake was to come the following day to take her back to Cape Town. And the certainty that she didn't want to see him, to be alone with him, so soon. I don't ever want to be alone with him again, she told herself defiantly.

She was glad that it was Saturday, that Cathy was at home, for the time passed more easily with the little girl's chatter and her laughter. When Philip came back from his office in the afternoon, Cathy insisted on her mother and father and Joanna sitting on the stoep to watch her riding round the lawn on her pony.

With Jannie walking beside her, holding the leading reins, she went round the lawn twice, the white pony moving slowly as if he were being extra careful of the child on his back.

'I could go faster,' Cathy called. 'Snowball would like to go just a little faster.'

'Careful, Cathy, you'll fall,' Philip said, standing up as the pony began to trot, not fast but undoubtedly beyond his stately walk.

And a moment later she did.

Philip ran down the steps but she was already picking herself up cheerfully, unhurt.

'I told you, Cathy, no trotting yet,' her father said angrily. 'Are you sure you're all right?' He turned to the young boy. 'Jannie, I said you weren't to let the pony trot. He's only to walk when you're in charge.'

'Cathy said she wanted to go faster,' Jannie protested. 'And she's good, Mr Sullivan, her hands are good on the reins.'

'It doesn't matter how good she is,' Philip returned brusquely. 'You do what I tell you, not what Cathy tells you.' He looked down at his small daughter. 'That's all for today, Cathy. Jannie will take Snowball back to the stables. And no more thinking you know best.'

'But, Daddy—' Cathy began, but Philip had turned away, leaving her to follow him.

'She's bound to fall, Philip,' Alice said when he sat down again. 'And she's not hurt—she never rides without her hat.'

'She's not to take chances like that,' Philip said, his mouth tight.

Fortunately, Joanna thought, and she could see that Alice was thinking the same, there was a phone call for Philip soon after that, and he had to go inside to take it.

Obviously, with Cathy beside them, there was nothing Alice could say, and perhaps that was just as well because it seemed to Joanna that Philip wasn't going to change, and that his attitude would make things more and more difficult for Alice as Cathy grew older. Unless Alice herself was to take a stand, and that didn't seem too likely.

Jake phoned that night and Alice, who had taken the call, came through to the dining-room, where they were having coffee.

'Jake is so sorry, Joanna,' she said, wheeling herself up

to the table. 'He has an unexpectedly long theatre list on Monday, and he won't be able to come through. He says he'll see you soon, and you're not to work too hard when you go back.' She turned to Philip. 'I said we'd get Joanna back. Can you manage, Philip?'

Philip shook his head.

'I'm in court all day Monday, but Bob is going through in the morning, isn't he?' He turned to Joanna. 'Bob Steyn is our farm manager—he'll take you through. The only thing is, he'd probably be going pretty early.'

'That's fine with me,' Joanna replied, meaning it. 'I'll need the day to get myself organised, ready for going back to work.'

A drive through with Philip, after the things he had told her, would have been difficult and awkward, she knew. But most of all she was extremely relieved that Jake wasn't able to come.

She didn't know what she was going to say to him when she did see him. But slowly, through the rest of that day and through the night, she came to see that what Philip had told her about Jake and Alice had been a confidence that wasn't hers to mention. In any case, she felt too sick at heart to want to hear anything Jake might have to say, especially when she thought of how sorry she had felt for him when he'd said he didn't know why the boyhood closeness between Philip and himself had gone. She didn't want to hear him mention Philip, or Alice.

If I could just never see him or hear of him again, that would be the best thing, she told herself as she was putting her things in her small suitcase. Because of their work at the hospital, that was impossible. For a few black moments, during the night, she had seriously wondered if she should leave, if she should either go back to London or go somewhere else in South Africa. But why should she let a man like Jake O'Connor spoil the dream she had had for so long of working at Groote Schuur?

'I'm not too happy about you going back to work tomorrow, Joanna,' Alice said worriedly when Joanna got into the estate car beside the farm manager. 'You have these dark shadows under your eyes.'

'I didn't bring enough make-up with me,' Joanna replied with a determined effort to sound cheerful. She bent and hugged the blonde girl. 'Alice, I don't know how to thank you for all you've done for me.' She straightened and turned to Anna, standing beside Alice's chair, her arms folded, a frown on her usually smiling face, and she hugged her, too. 'And you, Anna, you really did wonders for me. Your hot lemon drinks—your chicken soup—the way you looked after me.'

'But you don't listen, Miss Joanna,' Anna said sternly. 'Like I say, you should stay one day more—two days more, maybe.'

'I wish I could,' Joanna replied, not entirely truthfully. 'Alice, say goodbye to Cathy and Philip for me.'

The big, grey-haired farm manager was a man of few words, and she was glad of that, although in some ways talking would have kept the memories of previous journeys at bay. That first time, when they had had to stop because of the storm and Jake had held her in his arms and comforted her. And when they'd gone back after the Christmas visit, with the memory of that moonlight swim, of those moments in each other's arms—

Stop it, she told herself severely. It's over.

Over before it really began.

She shut that thought down smartly.

It was a little strange at first, being back in the old house she had just been beginning to think of as home. But when

Rose came off duty, and then Dorothy, and even David, busy as he always was, and the four of them had time for once to sit together at the big kitchen table and share some of the chili con carne Rose had made, Joanna began to feel that she did belong here.

'Must have been pretty good, being looked after so well in a real homestead like that,' Dorothy said with some envy when Joanna had told them about Anna and her lemon drinks and her chicken soup.

'For the first couple of days I felt so awful I couldn't really appreciate it,' Joanna told her, with perfect truth. 'But, yes, it was pretty good. And it certainly is a lovely house, and they were so kind to me.' She looked at her friends. 'But I was a visitor. I was on the outside of their lives, looking in. Here, it's different.'

She smiled.

'That sounds a bit lame, but I guess you know what I'm saying.'

'I think you're saying you like us, and you like living here,' Dorothy said briskly. She leaned forward, her elbows on the table, her chin in her hands. 'And now tell us about you and Dr Heart-throb O'Connor.'

Joanna felt her throat tighten.

'There isn't anything to tell,' she said, knowing she sounded brusque.

Dorothy shook her head.

'Come on, now,' she said, reproachfully. 'I saw him carry you through to your room when you fainted in his arms, I saw him sitting here for hours beside your bed. You can't tell me that means nothing!'

Joanna stood up.

'Yes, I can,' she said, her voice low. 'I'm telling you here and now it means nothing. I—won't be seeing him again, other than at work.'

'Have you had a quarrel?' Dorothy asked. 'Can't you make it up?'

'We haven't had a quarrel,' Joanna replied. 'There isn't anything to make up—there never was.'

'But—' Dorothy began.

'Leave it, Dorothy,' David said, with surprising authority.

Simultaneously, Rose said, 'For heaven's sake, Dorothy, don't be so nosy!'

Absurdly, Joanna felt her eyes fill with tears.

'Sorry, Dorothy,' she said, not quite steadily. 'I really don't want to talk about it any more.'

It was a disturbing thought, though, that although she could say that to her friends, and they would leave it at that, there was still Jake himself to face. She dreaded meeting him, for he would surely know right away that something was wrong, that something had changed.

The next morning, when he had finished his ward round and she had accompanied him because Sister Kenton was off duty, she found his dark blue eyes resting on her, questioning, as she made notes of the special instructions he gave her.

The young staff nurse was in the duty room and, as usual, she had a cup of coffee ready for Jake.

'Thanks, Nurse,' he said, and he sat down. 'Sister Boyd, I hope you're feeling fully recovered now?'

'Thank you, Dr O'Connor, I am,' Joanna replied, and she willed the young nurse to stay there, not to leave her alone with Jake.

'You'll let me know if Mrs Tembo's blood pressure rises, Sister,' Jake said. 'I'd like it monitored four-hourly.'

'Certainly, Dr O'Connor,' Joanna replied. 'I've made a note of that.'

A bell rang from one of the wards, and her heart sank as the young staff nurse hurried out.

Jake put his cup down on the desk.

'Is there something wrong, Joanna?' he asked. 'I'm sorry I couldn't manage to come and bring you back. Did Alice explain?'

'Yes, she did,' Joanna said. 'And of course I understood. It was no problem at all.'

'But there is something wrong,' Jake said levelly. 'I think we know each other well enough for me to realise that. I'll pick you up tonight, and we can talk about whatever the problem is.'

I have to do this now, Joanna told herself.

She took a deep breath.

'I don't think we really know each other at all, Jake,' she said. 'And I don't think there's any point in making any arrangements. There isn't anything we have to say to each other. Can we just leave it at that?'

He stood up, and his eyes were dark with anger, his lean brown face tight and controlled.

'I think you owe me some explanation, considering the way things were between us just a few days ago,' he said very quietly.

Joanna lifted her chin.

'I don't think I owe you anything,' she returned. 'And I'd rather forget what you just said.'

He looked down at her, unsmiling.

'If that's the way you want it,' he said.

She wouldn't let herself look away.

'That's the way I want it.'

For what seemed like an eternity his eyes held hers. Then, without another word, he turned and strode off down the corridor, away from her.

* * *

'I'm not being nosy, and I know you don't want to speak about him,' Dorothy said. 'I just want to know if there's anything I can do to help.'

Joanna managed to smile. Each in their own way, her housemates were being so caring, so supportive. Rose making tempting and tasty little treats for her, David putting up extra shelves for her in her room. And Dorothy. If looks could have killed, Jake would have dropped dead right there on the ward, Joanna sometimes thought, catching Dorothy glaring at him. From being top of the pops, his rating had gone way down.

'Thanks, Dorothy,' she replied. 'It's fine, really it is.'

It wasn't, and she could see that the younger girl knew this.

'I stuck around yesterday after that last delivery. I wasn't going to leave him alone with you,' Dorothy said fiercely.

And now Joanna's smile was real as she thought of Jake, weary after that long and difficult delivery, having a quick cup of coffee before responding to a call from one of the MOUs.

'Thanks, but I don't think I was in any danger,' she replied. 'And I don't think he wants to be alone with me, any more than I do with him.'

That, she was certain, was all too true. Jake was polite and professional and distant. And that's how I want it, Joanna reminded herself, thinking of him saying those very words to her.

A day or so later, she had just checked her labour room after a delivery, when Sister Kenton appeared.

'I'm trying to get hold of Dr O'Connor,' she said. 'We've just had a call from Hanover Park. They have an unbooked and, of course, undiagnosed multiple pregnancy. How any woman can ignore that is beyond me.

She should have been having regular check-ups, she should have been booked in here in good time, she should have...' She shook her head.

'Anyway, Sister Mtama out there sent for Flying Squad, and they're bringing her in.'

Twins, probably. Let's hope no more than that, Joanna thought as she ran over in her mind the possible problems. Unbooked, and with no monitoring of the mother's condition, so she could have any health problems from heart to kidneys or diabetes. The babies were almost certain to be premature, and the mortality rate for the second baby was always high. Malpresentation was more common, too.

'Two cots, with a third on standby,' she told Dorothy, glad that she was the staff nurse on duty. 'We have extra swabs, cord clamps, ligatures, mucus extractors. Phone Hanover Park and find out if they took blood—we should have cross-matched blood available in case it's needed.'

There was still no sign of Jake when the Flying Squad team brought their patient in, already in the third stage of labour. The room was warm, and there were extra blankets ready in case there was a degree of shock after the delivery.

'Why is there a danger of shock, Sister?' Dorothy asked, as Joanna checked the foetal heartbeats.

'Reduction in abdominal pressure. Check your Maggie Myles,' Joanna told her, intent on her patient. 'All right, Mrs Hendriks, relax in between. That's better—tensing won't help.'

And then there was no time to do anything but deliver the first baby, ligate the cord in two places and clear the baby's airway. Joanna left Dorothy to put the baby in the warm cot, and turned back to the mother.

'Oh, and make sure you label that baby number one,' she said, as she palpated to find the position of the second baby. Breech, she realised, dismayed, although she had half expected that.

'How are we doing, Sister?'

With relief, she heard Jake come in and stand beside her, putting on his rubber gloves while the student nurse tied his gown for him.

'First baby is fine, the second is breech,' she told him.

'Foetal heartbeat?' he asked.

'One-ten,' she told him.

For a moment, above their masks, his eyes met hers. They both knew that the second baby had to be born quickly or it was in trouble.

'Right, Mrs Hendriks, give us another good push,' Jake told the mother.

'I'm so tired, Doctor, I can't,' the woman in the bed protested.

'Nonsense, of course you can,' Jake told her, sympathetic but brisk. 'Come on, hold onto Sister here. That's it. Now another one.'

He was easing the tiny body now, and with a third push the baby was born, Jake's hands expertly easing the cord from the tiny neck.

'Baby number two,' he said, handing the baby, yelling now, to Joanna. 'And no more, thank heavens. A boy and a girl, Mrs Hendriks, and both all right. You're a lucky lady, I hope you realise that.'

A little later, as he and Joanna and Dorothy drank a quick cup of coffee, he said, 'No point in sounding off then about how foolish she was, not booking and not going for check-ups, but I will certainly have a few words with her before she goes. So many things could have gone wrong—she's darned lucky to have two healthy babies there.'

'And none too small either, for twins,' Joanna said.

'Both with good Apgars, too. And we were all lucky that she didn't have any problems herself,' she added soberly.

Jake put his mug down.

'Could have been worse, couldn't it?' he said cheerfully.

And then, as if he had just remembered, his face tightened and the cool distance returned to his eyes.

'Thanks, Sister, Nurse,' he said formally. 'You both did a good job.'

For a moment Dorothy's eyes met Joanna's as he turned and left them.

'He's still a good doctor, isn't he?' Dorothy said. 'The way he did that delivery, and kept the cord clear—pretty impressive, wasn't it?'

'Oh, yes, he's one of the best,' Joanna agreed, with complete certainty.

She picked up the chart she would have to fill in for Mrs Hendriks and her twins, all too conscious of the treacherous tightness in her throat, the sudden desolation at the change in Jake after the closeness of the difficult and successful delivery.

Joanna Boyd, you are a very foolish girl, she told herself severely. You can't have it both ways. You want him out of your life in a personal way, so you have to accept the way things are workwise.

In time it would surely become less hard. She would become so accustomed to this coolness between them that she wouldn't even notice it.

For one brief moment the thought was there, shocking her in its clarity. *Just who do I think I'm fooling?*

She'd had a phone call from Alice a few days after she'd gone back to work, asking how she was and passing on strict instructions from Anna about getting to bed early and having enough to eat. And the night after the delivery of the unbooked twins Alice phoned again.

'When are we going to see you, Joanna?' she asked. 'Are you off this weekend? And what about Jake—could you check with him, see when you're both off together?'

'I'm sorry, Alice, I'm on duty this weekend,' Joanna said, truthfully. 'I'll give you a ring next week maybe. I think I'd rather enjoy the drive out—my little car doesn't do much out in the country. But I'll let you know. How's Cathy?'

There was a short pause.

'She's fine,' Alice said, with care. 'Just a little frustrated because Philip doesn't want her to ride unless he's with her, after that fall.' She added, 'Do come soon, Joanna.'

Joanna promised that she would. But not, she knew, with Jake. That was something that sooner or later would come up again with Alice.

Was it strange, and was it wise, she wondered sometimes, that it was Alice, much more than Philip, who kept up the contact with Jake? And why did Philip allow it, feeling the way he did about his cousin? Then there was something else—why had Jake not kept his distance, perhaps even broken the contact, after the accident, knowing that Alice's decision had been to stay with Philip?

There was one bleak possibility that kept coming back to her, one answer to that last question.

Perhaps Jake couldn't keep away. Perhaps he still cared for Alice, cared for her so much that he'd rather see her on any terms than not at all. Perhaps it had suited him very well to have Joanna herself with him, to have Philip—yes, and perhaps Alice too—think that they were interested in each other.

He had said once that Alice wanted to find the right

girl for him. Perhaps Alice wanted that for her own peace of mind.

Perhaps...perhaps...

The only certainty, Joanna reminded herself firmly, was that she had been right to feel, from the start, that Dr Jake O'Connor wasn't to be trusted, that he was a man to keep well clear of. And as long as she remembered that she would be all right.

Except sometimes she woke to find her cheeks wet with tears, and her arms aching with the memory of how she had felt in his arms.

Absorbed in coming to terms with her own problems, it was with a sense of surprise one day that she realised that there was undoubtedly something in the air in the old stone house between Dorothy and David. Dorothy's eyes were starry, her cheeks were pink, David was more absent-minded than usual.

'No, he's fine at work,' Rose assured her, smiling, when she mentioned this, for she and David worked together in Casualty. 'It's just when he and Dorothy are near each other that he kind of loses it. I think it will be better for everyone when the two of them come clean—with each other and with everyone else!'

A few days later Joanna came home to find that this had happened.

'We're engaged,' Dorothy told her ecstatically. 'Look.'

It was an old ring, with tiny diamonds and garnets set into a wide band.

'I always wanted a Victorian ring,' Dorothy said. 'We found this in that antique shop on the main road. Isn't it beautiful?'

'It certainly is,' Joanna agreed, and she hugged Dorothy and then David. 'Congratulations, and I wish you both every happiness.'

'We can't afford to get married, but we probably will anyway,' the young doctor said cheerfully. He looked fondly at his very new fiancée. 'If we both move into Dorothy's room, because it's bigger, we could let my room.'

'We have to think about that,' Dorothy said. She turned to Joanna. 'Meanwhile, you're off on Saturday, aren't you? We're going to have a celebration, a beach braai at Camps Bay.'

The weather on Saturday was perfect, and as Joanna threaded meat on skewers, buttered rolls and made bowls of salad, she was looking forward to the evening. Afterwards, she wondered why she hadn't realised earlier that Jake would be there.

It was as they were packing picnic baskets that Dorothy mentioned it.

'David had to ask Jake,' she said hesitantly. 'They worked together before David moved to Casualty, and they were quite friendly. I didn't say anything before, because Jake thought he would be working, but he told David yesterday that he's managed to switch so...he'll be coming tonight. Do you mind very much, Joanna?'

'Of course not,' Joanna assured the younger girl. 'It's really nothing to me whether he's there or not.'

And that's perfectly true, she told herself. It was only a reasonable concern about any awkwardness that made her breath catch in her throat and her heart turn over when she and Dorothy reached the beach as the sun was setting, to find Jake there with David, helping to stoke the fire.

'Congratulations, Dorothy,' the big Irish doctor said. 'I don't have to call you Nurse Marais when we're all off duty, do I? I've just been telling David he's a lucky man.'

'We're both lucky,' Dorothy replied. With a quick, slightly worried glance at Joanna, she said, 'No, none of us are doctors or nurses or sisters tonight. Are we, Joanna?'

'Of course not,' Joanna said, and told herself that she wasn't going to do or say anything that might spoil this special time for her friends. Determinedly, she smiled at Jake, her head held high, in a challenge that she could see he recognised.

'So you two South Africans are going to teach foreigners like Joanna and me how to do this braai business, I suppose?' Jake said, and she could see with relief that he had accepted her challenge. 'And tell me, now, is the tradition that the men are to be looking after the fire and the meat, and you girls are clustered together checking out the salads? For I can tell you now, I like a bit of feminine company on a perfect evening like this. I don't fancy sharing a sunset so beautiful with a bloke like David here.'

Dorothy laughed, and Joanna could see that she was also relieved as she assured Jake that wasn't to be the way of it at all.

And it certainly wasn't, Joanna could see as the rest of the party arrived. Jake was immediately claimed and surrounded by nurses and sisters and a pretty red-haired doctor from Theatre. Not that Joanna herself was neglected, for Trevor, the accountant she had met at the house-warming party and had gone out with a couple of times, was obviously delighted to see her again. He had been on a skiing holiday, he told her. But now, apart from a couple of out-of-town audits, he was back in Cape Town.

The tantalising smell of the meat soon had everyone crowding round the fire as David set the food on one of the picnic tables they had brought with them. The sun had long since set, but the moonlight shimmered on the sea and the stars shone in a cloudless sky.

'Not quite like barbecues in England, is it, Jake?' the

doctor from Theatre said, and Jake agreed. 'Glad you came to Cape Town?'

For a moment, Joanna was certain, Jake's eyes met hers in the firelight. Mocking, challenging.

'Now, girl dear, and what do you expect me to reply to that?' Casually, he put an arm around her slim shoulders. 'Of course I'm glad, and not only for the weather—for the pleasure of working with girls like yourself.'

The red-haired woman shook her head.

'And what about the girls you left behind, you Irish heartbreaker?' she said, laughing.

All at once, Joanna had had enough. The girls he'd left behind? Helen Johnson, crying her heart out that day in the rose garden. And no sooner had he come here than he was making a play for his cousin's wife, taking advantage of her vulnerability.

Abruptly, she stood up and walked over to the small tables with the food. She put her plate down, and her glass of half-finished wine, and walked away from the laughing party into the welcome darkness of the beach. No one had noticed her going, she was sure as she heard the talk and the laughter behind her.

The sand was still warm on her bare feet, and the night was warm, and as she turned a corner the sounds of the party abated and she could hear the sea, breaking on the beach and on the rocks of the big rock pool.

Then, from the darkness, Jake appeared.

'Are you out of your mind, Joanna,' he said furiously, 'to be walking alone on the beach in the dark like this? And dressed the way you are. Are you looking for trouble?'

Joanna was completely taken aback. She was wearing her blue cotton sundress, with shoestring straps, but *dressed the way you are*?

'It's perfectly safe,' she returned, knowing she sounded defensive. 'I'm just round the corner from everyone else, and—and it's moonlight, and—'

'And it's a great night for vagrants, or teenagers out for mischief, or anyone at all, to see a woman on her own on a lonely beach.'

His tone was more brutal than his words, and she looked at him, more than a little shocked.

'I didn't think of that,' she admitted, her voice low. 'But surely this beach is safe?'

Unexpectedly, he sighed.

'It probably is,' he said, after a moment. 'I just...flipped when I saw you walk away, and disappear.'

Joanna remembered her earlier decision, that she wouldn't do or say anything that might spoil this special occasion for her friends.

'Did anyone else see me go?' she asked him. And then, recovering, she went on, 'Anyway, they might have thought I was going to the loo.'

'It's in the other direction,' Jake said. Of course, he was right—she remembered that now.

'Thank you, anyway,' she said stiffly, 'for coming after me. Even if it wasn't in the least bit necessary. Don't let me keep you from the party. I'll find my own way back.'

In the moonlight, he looked down at her, unsmiling.

'You damned well will not,' he said. 'You'll come back with me now.'

Anger flared in her.

'You have no right to give me orders, Jake O'Connor,' she told him.

His hands gripped her shoulders, hard.

'Oh, don't I know that, Joanna Boyd? But you don't have to be so damned foolish, as well as stubborn,' he said, his voice rough.

She could hear his breath coming unevenly, and she could feel her own heart thudding. She knew that she should move away, but she stayed where she was.

He kissed her then, his lips demanding, urgent at first with anger. And then the anger between them was gone, and there was nothing but the two of them alone on the beach, swept by a tide of passion more powerful than the tide of the Atlantic Ocean so close to them. A tide that there was no holding back.

The sand was still warm when at last Joanna became conscious of it on her shoulders, her legs.

In the moonlight, Jake's face was very close to hers.

'I should say I'm sorry,' he said unevenly. 'But that would be untrue.' Then, very gently, he touched her lips with one finger.

'Oh, Joanna, Joanna. What went wrong between us?'

Joanna drew back from him. She sat up and straightened her clothes. One strap had come off her shoulder, and she put it back in place.

'If you don't know,' she said, 'I don't feel like telling you.' And then, perversely and not quite steadily, she went on, 'But you should know. You should know why I feel the way I do about you.'

In the moonlight, his eyes were very dark.

'And you should know the way I feel about you,' he said, his voice taut. 'So this hasn't made any difference?' he asked her.

'No, it hasn't. Did you think it would?' she flung back at him, hardly knowing what she was saying, knowing only that this shouldn't have happened. She shouldn't have let it happen.

Now she could see that he was angry. Very angry.

'That wasn't why it happened, and you know that,' he said.

There was no reply she could make to that. She got up and walked back along the beach, back towards the fire and the people.

And away from Jake O'Connor.

CHAPTER SEVEN

No one made any comment when Joanna reached the noisy, happy group. She was too sick at heart even to be grateful for that. And she never knew how she got through the rest of the evening.

It was only later, back at home, that Dorothy said cautiously, 'I realised that you weren't there for a time, and neither was Jake. Were you together?'

Joanna felt as if the experience of that eternity on the beach was written on her face. But she managed to turn away and pick up a clean dishtowel to dry some more glasses before she replied.

'You didn't check who else was missing at the time, did you?'

It wasn't an answer, she knew that, and she could see that so did Dorothy. But the younger girl didn't press her any further.

She dreaded seeing Jake at work but, as she had found before, he was as able as she was to keep a cool and professional distance. They worked well together, and Joanna appreciated that there was no change in that. A difficult delivery—an unexpected Caesarean—a kidney patient he wanted admitted for observation. She could see each day that he depended on her to carry out his instructions, to anticipate his wishes, and she was glad of that. It was all she wanted from him, she told herself. And all he wanted from her, she was certain.

Which was why she was completely taken aback one

evening to answer the doorbell at the house and find him standing there.

'I have to talk to you,' he said brusquely. Then, perhaps seeing her immediate reaction, he said, 'About Alice.'

He looked down at her, unsmiling.

'Are we going to stand here talking, or may I come in? You're not in any danger from me, although you may find that hard to believe.'

Warm colour rose in her cheeks, and without a word she opened the door wider and led the way in. None of the others were at home, and she was glad of that.

He didn't sit down.

'The top neurosurgeon here, Brian Bristow, is leaving soon to go to America,' he said. 'He's the one who should do the operation that could let Alice walk again. I've spoken to him before and he's seen the X-rays, he's been through the whole medical background. He phoned me to tell me he's going, and to say that he will operate on Alice before he goes if an angiogram shows that her heart would stand up to it.'

His dark blue eyes held hers.

'I want you to talk to Philip, Joanna, to persuade him. Alice refuses to go ahead without him agreeing. I've talked to her and she would be prepared to risk it, but only if Philip agrees. I...can't talk to him. I don't know why, but that's how it is. He closes up, he behaves as if we were strangers and as if I have no right to step into his private life.'

The words were out before she could stop herself.

'And you do have that right?'

He stared at her.

'Of course I do. I can't stand by and let Alice lose this chance of walking again, of having a real life, of getting out of that wheelchair. For her, for Cathy—for Philip himself. So, will you try to persuade him, Joanna? For Alice's sake?'

She turned her head, looking away.

'I don't know if it would do any good,' she said, her voice low. But even as she said it she knew that she would have to try. As he'd said, for Alice's sake, for Cathy's sake.

'Don't count on anything,' she said. 'But...all right, I'll try.'

Taking her by surprise, he smiled, the warm smile she hadn't seen for so long, it seemed.

'Thank you for that, Joanna,' he said quietly. 'Will you let me know?'

She said that she would. At the door he looked down at her. For a moment he hesitated, as if he was going to say something, and then he walked down the path, out of the gate and into his car.

There was clearly no time to waste, although she had no idea how she would manage to talk to Philip alone. But she phoned Alice right away, and asked if she could come for the day on Saturday. Her friend's delighted response made her ashamed that she had been putting this visit off.

Cathy and Simba were waiting for her as she drew her little car up on the gravel. Philip and Alice were on the stoep.

'Just in time for coffee, Joanna,' Alice said, as Joanna bent and hugged her. 'Yes, you do look so much better. Just as well, Anna has been full of foreboding about you going back to work too soon.'

She poured coffee, and Joanna sat down at the wicker table. Cathy sat down on her small chair, and with a quick glance at her mother she said, 'You know what, Joanna?

My friend Julie Morton's mummy wants me to go with them to their beach house in Hermanus next weekend. They have such fun. The children sleep in a big room up in the roof and—'

'Cathy,' Philip said warningly, 'you know I said we'd talk about it later.'

'That means I can't go,' Cathy said flatly.

'We'll see,' her father replied. 'But surely you wouldn't want to leave Simba for three whole days? He'd be very lonely.'

'No, he wouldn't,' Cathy said, her lower lip turned down. 'He likes being with you and Mummy. Or maybe he could come too. Julie's dog Rufus always goes, and Rufus and Simba really like each other. They were both awful sorry that time they fighted.'

'Fought,' Philip said. 'Let's leave it for the moment, Cathy.'

Somewhat mutinously, the little girl seemed to realise she had better do just that. They had lunch on the stoep, and afterwards Philip gently and tenderly lifted Alice from her wheelchair to the comfortable couch. As he placed a cushion behind her head she looked up at him and smiled. And Joanna's breath caught in her throat. Whatever problems there had been between these two in the past, whatever difficulties there still were, one thing was absolutely clear—and that was the love there was between them.

'It's been so hot,' Alice said drowsily. 'I know I'm going to close my eyes. Philip, why don't you take Joanna to see the orchard? It's looking so pretty now. No, Cathy, you can stay here to keep me company.'

She knows, Joanna thought. She knows that Jake has asked me to talk to Philip.

Surprisingly, Philip didn't seem to find anything strange

in Alice's suggestion, and he and Joanna went off across the wide lawn towards the orchard.

'How do you think Alice is looking?' he asked, as they reached the shade of the trees.

Joanna hesitated.

'All right,' she said, after a moment. 'But...perhaps she's a little tired? She seems to be quieter than usual.' She took a deep breath. 'Philip, there's something I want to talk to you about—it's to do with Alice.'

She could see the guard go up in his face, in his eyes, immediately, but now that she had started she went on, telling him about the neurosurgeon leaving, pointing out that this was a chance for Alice that she shouldn't turn down.

'I know it must be a frightening thought for you—the possible risk—but surely you have to find out just what this problem is, if it really does make the operation too much of a risk.'

'I do know about this angiogram,' Philip replied, and the cool rejection in his voice made her heart sink. 'I've talked to quite a few doctors about it, and they all say it's an invasive procedure with a definite risk factor. You seem to know a great deal so you probably know the details of the heart problem. She has abnormal ECGs, she sees a specialist every six months and there was a suggestion that she should be on a beta blocker, but that was risky. And you talk about an operation!'

She couldn't feel angry with him—it was love and concern that made him say these things. She put one hand on his arm.

'Philip, right now all we're talking about is checking out this heart problem. It could be something easily put right, something that wouldn't present a problem in an operation.'

Philip turned away, but not before she had seen the closed tightness of his face.

'I can't risk losing her,' he said evenly.

There's nothing more to say, Joanna thought. He's not going to change his mind. But she had to keep on trying.

'Don't you want Alice to walk again?' she asked him. 'Do you want to keep her dependent on you for the rest of her life? Can't you just give her this chance, Philip?'

Without another word he turned and walked back to the house, stopping only at the foot of the steps to turn to her.

'Please, don't talk to Alice about this,' he said curtly.

And through the rest of that day he made sure that there was no chance for her to do that, never leaving Alice and her alone, making certain that either he or Cathy was with them all the time. There was only one moment, when Joanna was leaving, that Alice caught her hand.

'Thanks for trying, Joanna,' she whispered. 'It's all right—really it is.'

No, it isn't all right at all, Joanna thought sadly as she drove back to Cape Town. It could well be that the angiogram would have shown that the operation was too big a risk, but surely Philip could see that having it done would prove that, one way or the other.

'It wasn't any good. Philip just says he can't risk losing her—the angiogram is too risky,' she told Jake the next day in a quiet moment in the duty room after his ward round.

The big Irish doctor sighed.

'Yes, it's a risk,' he agreed. 'No one has ever tried to minimise that. But the bottom line is that there's just no question of an operation being done without the finding from an angiogram, and if Philip won't agree to that, Alice will never even have the chance to walk again.' He finished the coffee she had given him and stood up, once again the cool, professional doctor. 'Thanks for trying.'

And that's the end of it, Joanna thought. The last chance for Alice.

But two nights later Rose called her to the phone. It was Philip.

'Joanna,' he said, 'I've been thinking, since you talked to me. In all these years I have never allowed myself to remember the way I felt, right after the accident, when I heard that Alice might not walk again. But you made me remember, you made me face up to it.'

He hardly seemed to notice that he didn't give her time to reply.

'I was, of course, appalled. But just for a moment, I couldn't help thinking, Now she can't leave me. And when the heart business turned up, an operation really did seem too much of a risk. I mean that, Joanna.'

'I know you do, Philip,' Joanna replied quietly.

'But, after talking to you, I kept on thinking about it. And you're right. Alice has to have this done. We have to find out exactly what the problem is, what the risks are. And…take it from there.'

'Our heart unit is superb, Philip,' Joanna said. 'They have the most advanced techniques, and they know the risks with an angiogram—they'll look after Alice.'

She hesitated.

'Do you want to talk to Jake, or would you like me to ask him to make the arrangements?'

'I'd rather you did, if you don't mind,' he replied, as she had expected him to. And although part of her wanted nothing to do with the Irish doctor that wasn't strictly about the work they shared, there was a tiny, swiftly silenced part that couldn't help a treacherous moment of—

was it pleasure, was it pain? She didn't know, and she didn't want to know.

The next day, when she told Jake about Philip's phone call, his professional distance slipped for a moment. Did he, too, have mixed feelings? she couldn't help wondering. But what a foolish, unprofitable thought. Whatever he felt was of absolutely no interest to her, she reminded herself.

'You did it, you got him to change his mind,' he said, and he smiled. 'You're a star!' Then, brisk and cool again, he said he would make the arrangements.

'Fortunately, I can pull a few strings.'

Which he did, with good effect, for two days later Philip brought Alice in to see one of the cardiac specialists. Joanna, as soon as she was off duty, joined Philip in the waiting-room.

After what seemed like an eternity the door opened, and the grey-haired specialist, whom Joanna knew by sight, beckoned to Philip. And to Joanna.

'Alice's friend—Sister Boyd? Alice would like you to come in too.'

Alice looked a little white and anxious, but she managed to smile.

'Now,' Mr Morton said, sitting down at his desk, 'I'll be as brief and as non-technical as I can. Yes, we do have an abnormal ECG here, but there are other aspects that puzzle me. Alice has no chest pain and no breathlessness. I would have expected either or both of those. This test, an angiogram, involves injecting a special dye into the veins and tracing its progress through the whole body. That will identify the problem.'

For a moment, his eyes met Joanna's, as one professional to another.

'As I've explained, there's an element of risk in any

invasive procedure such as this. The risk isn't high, but I can't say there's no risk. Sister Boyd, I've been explaining to Alice that this is not done under an anaesthetic. She has to be conscious because every so often we tell her to take a deep breath while the dye is filmed. She would like you to be there. Sister Kenton is an old friend of mine—I'll have a word with her.'

Joanna went down to the car park with Philip and Alice, and when Alice was settled in the seat she leaned out and put her hand over Joanna's.

'I can't say I'm not nervous about this, but it will help, having you there, Joanna.'

It was strange, putting on full theatre gown, cap and boots, Joanna found, for it was years since she'd had theatre experience.

'Mr Morton says you can stand here, and you'll see the screen and Mrs Sullivan can see you,' the senior theatre sister told her briskly as Alice was brought in on a trolley, a little drowsy because she'd been given a pre-med to sedate her.

'Hi,' she said, her face lighting up when she saw Joanna. 'Pretty impressive, this.'

The huge camera was positioned above her, and when Mr Morton came in, gowned and capped, he told her that he was going to make a small groin incision and insert the dye.

'You might feel a slightly unpleasant sensation as it goes into your veins,' he told her. 'I'll ask you from time to time to take a deep breath so that we can take a still.'

It was a strange feeling for Joanna, being there but not part of the theatre team. Once or twice she saw Alice's eyes widen and she smiled reassuringly, hoping Alice could see the smile above the mask. She glanced at the monitor screen, not fully understanding but fascinated. The whole procedure seemed to take a long time, and when it was over she realised how stiff she was from standing still so long.

Alice was taken back to the ward, where she had to lie still for the rest of the day because of the incision. Joanna looked in when she could, and she was there when Mr Morton came in, late in the afternoon.

'I'm sorry your husband isn't here, Alice,' he said, brisk but smiling, 'because I have very good news for you. There isn't anything wrong with your heart.'

'But the abnormal ECGs?' Alice asked.

'Very rarely,' the doctor said, 'we get what we call a false positive. That means that all your ECGs show this abnormal pattern when there is, in fact, nothing wrong. I had a suspicion that this might be the case with you, but I didn't want to raise your hopes. And this was the only way we could be certain.'

He patted Alice's hand.

'I'm very pleased, my dear, to be telling you this. You'll be seeing Mr Bristow very soon to discuss an operation?'

'I— Yes, I suppose so,' Alice said, dazed. 'My husband and I will have to talk about it, now that we know this.'

When the specialist had gone, Joanna turned to Alice.

'Jake will arrange it for you,' she said. 'Will Philip mind that?'

Alice's blue eyes were steady.

'I don't know,' she admitted. Then her chin rose. 'But he'll have to live with that. And who knows, maybe if this operation is successful, if I can walk, Philip and Jake can put the clock back and be friends again.'

I wouldn't count on that, Joanna thought when she left Alice's room, remembering the bitterness in Philip's eyes and voice when he'd told her that Jake had been the man Alice had loved, the man she'd thought of leaving him for. Perhaps Alice could put that behind her, and go on. Perhaps even Jake could. But she didn't think that Philip would find that easy at all.

She knew that Jake would hear the good news, either from Alice herself or from the cardiac specialist, and he would surely speak about it when he came to do his ward round the next day. And when this was all over, she thought, Alice's operation and the contact because of it, they would go back, he and she, to the way they'd been, to their cool professional relationship.

But that night, when she got home, there was a letter waiting for her, a letter that was to shatter that certainty and make her rethink all she had ever known about Jake.

'Letter for you from England,' Dorothy said, coming in with the mail. 'One of your old buddies?'

Joanna looked at the name and address on the back.

'Yes, a female buddy,' she told her friend. 'Pat Hale—she and I nursed together at St Margaret's.'

She poured herself a cup of tea, and sat down on the swing seat on the stoep with her letter. News of the awful weather they'd been having—the Christmas dance—the staff changes. It all seemed like another world, Joanna thought.

Then she came to the final paragraph.

And here's something that will surprise you. Remember Jake O'Connor and Helen Johnson? Remember how mad we all were when he ditched her? Well, do I have news for you. Here's the reason he broke their engagement. I heard this from Helen's cousin, who's just come here from Bart's. Jake found out that she was having an affair with Dick Kennedy from Orthopaedics—married, two kids, one of them Down's. Apparently our Jake was so furious with Helen for breaking up the marriage that he called off their engagement, which, let me tell you, Helen had been using as a cover for her affair. So I guess we were all a bit quick and a bit harsh, judging him. Thought you'd be interested.

Interested?

More, much more than that.

Joanna folded the letter slowly.

I was wrong about him, she thought painfully. No wonder he said I had been very quick to judge him, without really knowing.

And there was another thought, even more devastating. If she had been wrong about Jake and Helen Johnson, could she have been wrong—could Philip have been wrong—about Jake and Alice? Joanna suddenly remembered clearly what Philip had said.

'It was Jake, of course…she didn't have to say his name. There wasn't time then because that was when the tractor turned in front of us.'

Alice hadn't said it was Jake.

I have to know, Joanna thought. I have to know, and so does Philip.

Deep shame filled her at her unquestioning acceptance of what Philip had told her. She didn't even wonder—then or later, she came to realise—why she could so quickly come to the conclusion that Philip had been wrong, that she had been wrong, about Jake and Alice. It wasn't just because of the letter. It was, perhaps, something deep inside herself. Because she wanted the man Alice had loved not to be Jake?

She didn't know how or when she would be able to see Philip on his own to tell him that. It didn't seem the sort of thing she could talk to him about on the phone. She did phone Alice the next day to see how she felt after the angiogram and to ask about the operation.

'Next week,' Alice told her. 'We saw the neurosurgeon this morning. He said I needed a few days after the angiogram, but he wants to do it as soon as possible so that he can monitor my progress before he leaves for America.' She laughed, a little shakily. 'I liked hearing him say "progress", Joanna, but, of course, I'm not counting on anything. I have to go in early the day before, he says, so that he can have all the necessary tests done. Will you come and see me then?'

'Of course I will,' Joanna promised.

And, of course, Jake will, too, she thought, and if I don't speak to Philip soon, just knowing Jake is likely to see Alice will have Philip putting up that cold front, and any upset like that is the last thing Alice needs at this stage.

Jake himself, apart from a brief comment that he supposed Joanna knew about Alice's operation, said no more to her than their professional interaction required, other than once saying to her, 'Are you all right, Sister Boyd?' Her immediate reply in the affirmative got a nod, and that was all. But she found herself looking at him with new eyes, with new knowledge. Knowledge that she would have given anything to have had before.

The day before Alice's operation, Joanna went to see her during her lunch-hour. Alice was sitting up in bed, the blue velvet band Joanna had given her keeping her fair, curly hair back from her face. She looked well, Joanna thought, but a little anxious. Philip was with her, looking out the window, and he turned when Joanna went in.

'I knew you'd be here soon,' Alice said. 'I just hoped

you knew the hospital well enough to find me—I hadn't realised it was quite as huge.'

'And the orthopaedic floor is miles from us on Maternity,' Joanna told her. She hugged the girl in the bed. 'I suppose they're keeping you busy with tests?'

'Lots of them,' Alice agreed. 'Mr Bristow says he isn't taking any chances.'

'He's very thorough,' Philip said, a little grudgingly.

Joanna sat down, and they talked for a little longer, Alice expressing her concern about Cathy and her reaction to the news of the operation.

'I'll give her a ring tonight, see if I can help at all,' Joanna said. She was wondering if there was any possibility of getting Philip away when the staff nurse came in, a syringe in her hand.

'I'm sorry, Mrs Sullivan,' she said briskly. 'We need more blood, but this is the last of the tests. No, you don't have to go, Mr Sullivan, this will only take a minute.'

'The grapes, Philip, in the car,' Alice said. 'We brought grapes for you, Joanna, and some for Jake. Go down with Joanna now, Philip, and give them to her, and you could bring the ones for Jake up here. I'm sure he'll come in to see me.' She smiled at the staff nurse. 'And the rest are for you folks up here so bring them up, too, Philip.'

It was only when they were out of the busy, bustling hospital and in the car park that Joanna could take her chance.

'I have to talk to you, Philip,' she said, as he unlocked the Range Rover. She took a deep breath, and then, very steadily, she told him about the letter she had just had, telling her the truth about Jake's broken engagement in England.

'I just assumed—we all did—that he had jilted Helen, that he was to blame,' she said. She looked up at him. 'I was wrong about that, Philip, and I wonder if perhaps you've been wrong, assuming that Jake was the man Alice was in love with.'

Philip shook his head.

'Oh, no,' he said vehemently. 'I'm not wrong, Joanna. Of course it was Jake.'

'She didn't say it was Jake,' Joanna reminded him, and now she saw just a flicker of doubt on his face. She put her hand on his arm. 'Philip,' she said urgently, 'you have to know the truth. I have to know the truth.'

He didn't question her right to the truth, she realised afterwards.

'You'll have to find out from Alice,' she said, before that doubtful expression disappeared. 'So that you and Alice can go on from here. But do it carefully, Philip. If you've been wrong for all this time, Alice mustn't know that you've thought it was Jake.'

Philip's grey eyes were clouded.

'And if I haven't been wrong?' he asked her.

Joanna lifted her chin.

'Then we'll know for sure, won't we?' she said, her voice low.

It was only later, when she was alone, that she could admit the questioning thought that had been there, deep down, from the time she got the letter. What good would it do her, whichever way this turned out? Jake and her. Only…there wasn't any Jake and her, together. She had effectively put an end to any possibility of that when she'd accepted so quickly what Philip had said.

She phoned Cathy, and told the little girl she had been to see her mother in hospital.

'Daddy will bring me to visit Mummy after the operation is over,' Cathy said. 'But he says it might be quite a long time before Mummy comes home.' She sighed. 'I don't like Mummy being away, Joanna, and neither does Simba.'

Joanna thought for a moment.

'Here's an idea, Cathy,' she said. 'Ask Daddy to let you have a calendar in your bedroom, and every day, when you go to bed, you can put a big cross—maybe a big red cross—through that day. Then, when the doctor says when Mummy can come home, you could put a big red circle round that day, and you'll see the crosses coming closer to the big red circle.'

There was a long silence.

'I think me and Simba would like to do that,' Cathy said at last, cautiously.

'Goodnight, Cathy,' Joanna said. 'Here's a kiss—can you hear it?'

The little girl giggled.

'I did hear something funny. Goodnight, Joanna.'

There was no chance for her to see Alice before the operation the next morning, but through her own busy morning her thoughts kept going to the theatre and the team who would be working on Alice. And Philip, waiting.

'Take an extra half-hour for your coffee-break, Sister Boyd,' Sister Kenton said kindly. 'Pop over and see how things are going. I do think we're in for a quieter time now, with these four deliveries over.'

Philip was in the waiting-room, a magazine open in front of him. It was a moment or two before he saw Joanna, although she walked over and stood in front of him.

'She's been in for hours,' he said without preamble. He looked weary, exhausted, and in spite of everything Joanna's heart went out to him.

'I'll see if I can find out how much longer it will be,' she said, and she went off to find the sister in charge of the theatre list.

'At least another hour,' she told Philip when she came back. 'Have you had anything to eat this morning?'

He shook his head.

'It was so early when I left home that I didn't feel like having anything,' he said.

'Then we'll go to the cafeteria now,' Joanna told him firmly. 'It will do you more good than sitting here. Frankly, you look pretty awful—it wouldn't help Alice at all to see you like that.'

Philip managed an attempt at a smile.

'I can't argue with that,' he said. The smile disappeared. 'And I need to talk to you, Joanna.'

In the cafeteria, Joanna collected two coffees, and a cheese and ham sandwich for Philip. As he ate and drank, she waited, her heart thudding unevenly as she wondered what he was going to tell her.

'I talked to Alice last night,' he said at last, abruptly. 'I wasn't sure if I should, but you were right—I had to know.' His grey eyes were dark, shadowed. 'I don't know if I went about it the right way, but we were alone and it was quiet. I said to her, "Alice, if this operation is successful, if you can walk again, will it make a difference to us, to you and me? Will you want to make a new life for yourself, as you were planning to before the accident?"'

He was silent, for what seemed to Joanna like an eternity, but she forced herself to wait.

'She didn't even hesitate,' he eventually said wonderingly. 'She shook her head, and she said, "How could you think that, Philip? As soon as I could, after the accident, I wrote to John and told him it was over."'

'John?' Joanna repeated.

Philip's eyes were steady.

'I knew then, of course. John Kirby was a neighbour of ours. He was on his own, and he used to come over fairly often. I never for a moment thought... He sold his farm, moved away, soon after the accident. Now, when I look back, I can see...a great many things.'

Joanna leaned forward.

'But why were you so sure it was Jake?' she asked him.

Again, it was a long time before Philip replied.

'It wasn't when we were boys,' he said, slowly, painfully, looking down at his empty cup on the table. 'Everything was fine then. But later, when we were older, Jake was always the winner and I was the loser. He was the one girls fell for, he was the one who did so well at school, at sports. I was the quiet one, he was the one with all the charm. Oh, he didn't know, he didn't trade on it, but I knew. Maybe that was why I came out here, to get out from under his shadow. Then, when he came, too, I guess I expected that the pattern would be repeated. I suppose I expected to lose Alice to him, and so I saw things that weren't there, I made assumptions that I shouldn't have. I think, now, that he was just being his usual self, and Alice was just being friendly, welcoming, to my cousin.'

He lifted his head.

'And, of course, long before he came, there were problems between Alice and me. She said I was too possessive, she said I didn't give her any freedom. And she was right. I suppose that was when she found John sympathetic, understanding.'

He stood up.

'I can't wait here any longer,' he said brusquely. 'I have to get back up there.'

Joanna followed him out into the corridor, and to the

lift, her mind whirling. But there was no time even to take in all that he had said, all that it meant, for soon after they sat down again in the waiting-room Mr Bristow came in.

'She'll do,' he said, briefly, wearily.

Philip stood up.

'What do you mean?' he asked, his voice hoarse.

'I mean that, barring anything unforeseen, she should be able to walk again,' the surgeon told him, and now he smiled. 'The nerve damage was less than it might have been. It will take time, and she'll have a fair bit of pain in the early days, but the operation has been successful—I can definitely say that. You can see her in half an hour, although she's not likely to be fully conscious.'

'Will she know I'm there?' Philip asked.

'Yes, I think she will,' Mr Bristow replied, and he left them, a quick nod his acknowledgement of Philip's stumbling words of thanks.

Joanna left then and went back to the maternity block. She was there in time for Jake's ward round, and when he came into the duty room she could see that he had heard the good news.

'I just heard from Brian Bristow,' he said. 'Great news, isn't it? He said you were with Philip. He must be thrilled.'

'I don't think he's taken it in properly yet,' Joanna said. 'He looked exhausted.'

'Poor old Philip,' Jake said, with such real sympathy that Joanna found herself thinking how sad it was that all these misunderstandings had arisen between the two cousins.

Then, as if remembering that there should be coolness and distance between them, Jake's face became closed, all the warmth there had been in it gone.

'Anything particular to report, Sister?' he asked formally.

Joanna glanced at the charts she had ready.

'A rise in Mrs Temba's blood pressure,' she told him. 'And I'm not too happy about a lack of movement with Mrs Jonas. The foetal heartbeat is stable, but I'm not happy.'

'We'll check her right away,' Jake said. He smiled, but it was a brief, professional smile. 'I always like to accept an instinctive feeling like that—it's usually valid.'

And this time it certainly was. Jake decided to induce Mrs Jonas's baby, and Joanna found herself hanging on when she should have been off duty so that she could deliver the baby herself.

'He's fine,' she told the mother, as she wrapped up the yelling baby and put him in his mother's arms.

'I was worried when Dr O'Connor said he wanted to induce,' the young woman said. 'I thought there was something wrong with my baby.'

There might have been if he hadn't been induced, Joanna thought, once again grateful for Jake's professional skill, backing up her own instinct.

There was no time then for her to think about what Philip had told her. She went to look in on Alice when she finally came off duty, knowing that she would find her friend drowsy and sedated but wanting to see her, even briefly.

It was an odd feeling, seeing Alice lying white and still in Intensive Care. Somehow the tubes and the monitor screen, which Joanna was familiar with and which she should have found reassuring, seemed strange and threatening, when this was someone she was fond of.

'Joanna?' Alice murmured, opening her eyes. 'I sent Philip to get something to eat. He looks so tired.'

'I know,' Joanna said, for the sister in charge had told her. 'He should be back soon. Don't try to talk, Alice. Sleep if you want to. I'll stay until Philip gets back.'

Alice nodded drowsily. Joanna sat beside her as her eyes closed again, and by the time Philip came back she was soundly asleep.

It was a fortnight before Alice was allowed to go home. Joanna visited her every day, whenever she could. Philip came through in the evenings, and at the weekends he brought Cathy with him. By then Alice was out of Intensive Care and in a small side ward. Even so, Cathy was clearly not too happy, and Joanna took her to her own block to see the babies.

Sometimes when Joanna was with Alice, Jake came to see her. There was no doubt about his affection for his cousin's wife, but Joanna could see now, very clearly, that it was no more than that.

She had to talk to him, she knew that. She had to apologise, and she had to tell him what Philip had thought, why there had been this breach between them. If she didn't, they would never regain anything at all of the closeness they had once had. And she did owe him that.

Once, when Jake was leaving, she thought of going with him, of taking this chance. But her courage failed her when she saw the cool hostility in his eyes, resting on her briefly, as he turned to go.

Alice and Philip asked her if it would be possible for her to take a few days off and to come to Morgenster when Alice got out of hospital.

'Mr Bristow would like me to have a nurse, just for the first few days,' Alice said. 'I'd much rather it was you than someone I don't know. Anna wouldn't mind you looking after me, but she'd be pretty resentful of anyone else, I think.'

It wasn't difficult to arrange, and Joanna went with Alice in the ambulance that took her home.

'We look after Miss Alice together,' Anna said very firmly, and Joanna found that this worked very well. The woman's hands were strong and gentle as she and Joanna lifted Alice from the bed to the wheelchair, and then, after a few days, helped her into the pool, where the physiotherapist did the exercises Mr Bristow had given her.

And with each day, it seemed to Joanna, there was just a little improvement, a little less pain.

'I won't feel too bad, leaving you tomorrow,' she said to Alice, the day before she was to go back to Cape Town. 'Between Anna and your daily physiotherapy, you're doing pretty well.'

'I see Mr Bristow again next week,' Alice said. 'Progress report. Joanna, I don't think I can ever say just how grateful I am, to Jake and to you, for all you did. Maybe you, most of all, for talking to Philip and persuading him.' She hesitated. 'I do think things are doing to be different now between Philip and me. And for Cathy, too. Somehow I'm getting through to him that he has to let go, with both of us.' She smiled. 'We're talking, Philip and I, about perhaps having another baby. Mr Bristow says to give it time, but there's no reason why we shouldn't.'

'I think that would be the best thing, for all of you,' Joanna said, meaning it with all her heart.

She left Alice to have the afternoon rest she was supposed to have, and went downstairs.

And there, standing in the hall, was Jake.

'Anna said it's time for Alice's rest,' he said.

'Yes, it is,' Joanna replied. 'Just an hour, but she does need it. Do—do you want tea or coffee?'

'Anna has just taken some coffee out to the stoep. I think she's put out a cup for you as well.'

His voice was stiff and his eyes were cool as she went outside with him.

I don't want to do this, Joanna thought, but I have to.

'Jake,' she said, and she hoped her voice was steady. 'I have to talk to you.'

One dark eyebrow was raised, mocking and questioning.

'You do?' he said coolly. 'Sure and I can't think that there is anything that needs to be said between you and me, Joanna.'

Joanna took a deep breath.

'Oh, yes, there is, Jake,' she said. 'And the first thing is—I'm sorry.'

The dark blue eyes held hers. She knew that it was no use, knew by the cool remoteness in the way he looked at her.

'Whatever you're sorry for, my dear,' Jake said, 'is it not a little late for that?'

CHAPTER EIGHT

SOMEHOW Joanna managed to keep her voice steady.

'Yes, perhaps it is a little late to say I'm sorry,' she replied. 'But I have to say it. Jake, I had a letter from someone I nursed with at St Margaret's. She told me what really happened between you and Helen Johnson. Why you broke your engagement.'

It was a moment before he said anything.

'And, of course, what you hear from someone else has much more weight than any conclusions you might have drawn yourself about me.'

His voice was pleasant, reasonable. And so very cool.

'I said I'm sorry,' Joanna said again, her voice low.

'Of course you did,' Jake agreed. 'And that changes everything. I'm afraid all I can say is—and so?'

Her heart sank even farther. This wasn't going to be easy. Her pride almost made her give up, but she had to try again. Because this mattered so much more than any foolish pride.

'There's something else,' she said painfully. 'Something you don't know.'

Deliberately, the big doctor poured coffee, and handed hers to her.

'I can't wait to hear what else you have to tell me,' he said.

Something in Joanna snapped.

'Do you have to make this even more difficult for me than it already is?' she flung at him.

He was silent, and after a moment she went on slowly,

feeling for the right words, the words that would help him to understand what had come between himself and his cousin.

'You probably don't know that when the accident happened Alice and Philip were arguing. She has always felt that it was as much her fault as his. But it's more than that. She told him that he was too possessive, that he was smothering her, that she was thinking of leaving him.'

Now she had Jake's full attention, she could see that, as she went on.

'She told him that she was in love with someone else. Before she said his name the accident happened.'

She could see that he still didn't understand. She leaned forward.

'Jake, Philip thought it was *you* she was in love with, *you* she was going to leave him for. He has thought that all this time,' she told him. 'But he knows the truth now. He knows it wasn't you.'

'Why on earth did he think it was?' Jake said, bewildered. 'Did Alice tell him that?'

She shook her head. Carefully, she told him what Philip had told her about his perception of the years when the two cousins had been growing up. Jake the winner, and Philip the loser. And this time the prize had been Alice, and Philip had been certain that once again Jake had won.

Jake stood up and walked to the wall beside the step, staring out into the garden.

'How could I not have seen how he felt?' he said, more to himself than to her. 'At school—at university—I never thought of Philip seeing things that way. He was my cousin, my mate.'

There was nothing she could do or say. She waited, watching him, until at last he turned round. He had regained control of himself, but she could see that it had been an effort.

'I'm grateful to you for telling me this,' he said, courteously. 'Perhaps Philip and I can manage to rebuild something of what we once had.' He put his coffee-cup down on the table. 'If you don't mind, I think I'll go for a walk. I need to do some thinking. Will you tell Alice I'll be back soon?'

He had reached the steps before she managed to say anything, before she managed to crush the pride that was keeping her silent.

'Jake,' she said shakily.

He turned round.

She tried once more. 'I'm saying it again,' she said. 'I am so sorry.'

He shrugged. 'And I'm saying it again,' he returned. 'Surely it's a little late for that?'

She had to keep on trying, she knew that.

'I thought we had something, you and I,' she said, her voice low.

With two steps he was back beside her, his hands on her shoulders, hard and rough, as he looked down at her.

'Oh, yes, we did have something—you're right about that,' he said. He crushed her in his arms, and his lips found hers, savage and passionate. A kiss with no warmth, no tenderness. And yet, in spite of that, a kiss that once again made an answering passion surge through her whole body as he held her tightly.

Then he released her abruptly.

'Electricity, chemistry—whatever you want to call it—oh, yes, we did have something,' he said, and the contempt in his voice made her arms drop to her sides, made any movement towards him completely impossible. 'But these things aren't worth much, are they? A little trust, a little tolerance, a little less rushing to be judgmental—that's worth a heck of a lot more.'

He strode down the steps and across the sweep of lawn. Through a blur of tears Joanna watched him.

She didn't know how she got through the rest of the day. At times it seemed as if there were a glass wall between herself and the rest of the world. Alice, on the couch on the stoep, talking to Jake, telling him about the physiotherapy she was having. Cathy, home from school and full of excitement at finding Jake there. And Jake himself, talking to Alice, lifting Cathy high in the air.

They were all there, they were all real, but Joanna felt as if she wasn't part of any of it. Once or twice she found Alice's eyes resting on her, concerned. And when Jake had gone, saying he was sorry he couldn't stay until Philip came home but he would see him soon, Alice put one hand on Joanna's arm.

'You could have gone back with Jake today, Joanna, although it's no problem to take you back tomorrow. I was going to suggest that, but I felt it maybe wasn't a good idea.'

Joanna managed to smile.

'No, it wouldn't have been a good idea,' she admitted.

Alice hesitated.

'I did hope that something was developing between you and Jake,' she said carefully. 'But somehow, today, I got the feeling that things weren't too good.'

'You're right about that,' Joanna replied. And then, with a total disregard for truth, she said, lightly, 'It isn't important, Alice. Just...one of these things that didn't work out, that's all.'

'Perhaps you'll sort it out when you're back at the hospital and working together,' Alice said.

Joanna shook her head.

'I wouldn't count on that,' she said with certainty.

As she had expected, Jake was correct, professional and nothing more when she went back on duty two days later.

'We're all very glad to have you back, Sister Boyd,' Sister Kenton said that first morning when Jake arrived to do his ward round. 'Aren't we, Dr O'Connor?'

Jake busied himself checking one of the charts on the desk.

'Of course we are, Sister Kenton,' he agreed politely. And he led the way along the corridor and into the ward.

The next few days were as busy as usual, and Joanna was glad. The young mother Jake had told her about, who had had fertility treatment, was admitted so that she could be kept under observation. Joanna found herself taking a special interest in Pamela Sutton as the days went by.

'You're sure my babies are all right, Sister?' the mother asked anxiously each time Joanna checked the foetal heartbeats.

'Your babies are fine—three separate heartbeats, and each one strong,' Joanna always assured her.

When she had time she would sit down and talk—or rather let her patient talk.

'I'm thirty-five, you know—but, of course, you do know from my chart. And we were just about giving up when this last IV treatment worked. Dr O'Connor was marvellous. He's been a terrific support all the time to both of us.' She patted her abdomen, and smiled. 'I should say to the five of us.' Then, her smile gone, she said quietly, 'You know, Sister, when Dr O'Connor told us there were three babies, I was devastated. I couldn't think how on earth we would manage. Then, as the babies began to grow, I began to see how ungrateful that was. There we were, desperate for a baby, and we were being given the gift of three—and here I was, saying we couldn't manage! Of course we can—we won't have much money, but for sure we'll have enough love for our three babies.'

'Of course you will,' Joanna agreed, not quite steadily. She stood up. 'Coffee-break over, and we have two mums just about ready to deliver.'

'I wish it was me,' Pamela said. 'But, as Dr O'Connor keeps telling me, every day we keep my babies inside gives them a better chance when they do come out!'

And I hope I'm around when that happens, Joanna thought as she went back to the ward. Apart from the interest of seeing triplets delivered, she did want to be there when Pamela gave birth.

She went out to visit Alice on her next weekend off, and found her friend bright and positive, although she did admit that she got a little impatient with her slow progress.

'But at least it is progress,' she said. 'Philip tells me that, and so does Jake.' Her eyes met Joanna's. 'Jake was out last weekend, but he's on call this weekend so he won't be here.'

Alice is telling me I don't need to worry about that, Joanna thought. But she'd already known he wouldn't be here, because she'd checked the roster herself. Just as he probably had the previous weekend, she told herself, to make sure he wouldn't find me here.

Alice was talking about Jake and Philip now, about a change she thought she could see in Philip's attitude to his cousin.

'I don't suppose I'll ever know what the trouble was,' she said quietly, looking at Philip and Cathy, out on the lawn with Cathy's pony. 'Philip doesn't open up easily. But things have definitely changed in many ways since my operation, and perhaps this is another step forward. I wouldn't say they've got back to being really close, but there's a kind of thaw there now. Now, tell me what you've been doing, Joanna.'

'Delivering babies,' Joanna replied, laughing. 'And waiting for those triplets to be born.'

'Oh, yes, Jake was talking about them, too. But I mean in your off-duty time, not at work.'

'I've been to the theatre with the accountant I told you about,' Joanna said. 'And tomorrow night I'm going on a double date with Dorothy and David and one of the other doctors to the jazz restaurant at the Waterfront. And as for the rest of the time—believe me, Alice, when I've been on my feet all day I'm very glad to sit down, wash my hair, read a magazine, just relax and get ready for the next day.'

Which was all perfectly true, she told herself as she was driving home to Cape Town. And he was very nice, the accountant, and so was the doctor.

But they're not Jake, either of them.

The thought was there, clear and stark and inescapable.

I just need time, she told herself determinedly. Time to put this man right out of my mind.

And my heart.

Yes, she thought, with sadness. I have to put him out of my heart, too.

It seemed strange now that she had once thought she'd felt heartbroken when she'd found out about Cliff. Cliff? I didn't know what heartbreak was then, she thought. What had happened between Cliff and her had been nothing. Except—and the thought was very painful—if it hadn't been for Cliff, and what he had done, perhaps she would have been less ready to believe the worst of Jake.

A few days later Pamela Sutton went into labour. Joanna sent for Jake right away, as he had asked her to.

'Can't you stop it?' Pamela asked, her eyes wide and

anxious. 'I know you were hoping I'd go at least another fortnight.'

Jake shook his head.

'I'm afraid we can't stop it now, Pamela,' he said. 'Your babies are small, but they've got a good chance. Now, rest—you've got a long way to go.'

Back in the duty room, Jake's eyes were concerned.

'The babies are tiny,' he said. 'I can't risk her going fully into labour, and perhaps having a difficult birth that could put too much strain on these babies. I'm going to do a Caesarean. Sister Boyd, I know you're not on duty but I'd like you to assist, if you don't mind.'

'I'll be glad to,' Joanna said, meaning it. She did always enjoy working with Jake in the theatre, being part of the team, and she would have hated to have missed out on this birth.

The green-gowned figures moved swiftly around the theatre, each one knowing precisely what to do. The trolley was wheeled in, and Joanna managed a quick, reassuring word with Pamela, already very drowsy. The anaesthetist moved towards her, and a few minutes later the theatre doors swung open and Jake came in backwards, his gloved hands held high, his mask in place.

'Everything ready?' he asked, brisk and professional. 'ICU standing by for the babies? Good, let's get to work.'

He had a quick word with the anaesthetist, nodded his approval and then took the scalpel Joanna had ready for him. As always, the speed and precision awed Joanna as she watched him make the first incision. Then, unbelievably quickly, first one baby, then the second and then the third were delivered and handed to the waiting nurses. Jake did the first deep stitches to close the wound, and then the neat stitching of the final layer.

Only then did he lift his head.

'How are the babies?' he asked.

'Two of them are fine,' the Sister from ICU told him. 'Tiny, but colour good, breathing normal, no signs of distress. But the third one—I'm not happy about him. We're taking them off right now.'

She and her assistants wheeled the three small incubators out. For one moment, Jake's eyes met Joanna's above their masks in shared concern. Then Jake checked his patient again, spoke to the anaesthetist and left the theatre, with his usual quick word of thanks to his team.

Joanna didn't go off duty. She knew that Pamela would be conscious soon, if drowsy, and she wanted to see her. But before that she wanted to know how the babies were doing. She went along to the ICU, where the sister who had been in Theatre took her to the babies right away.

Joanna stood beside the incubators, and her breath caught as she looked at the tiny babies, naked, each one with a nasotracheal tube and the smallest one in a Vicker's incubator, with assisted ventilation.

'He's the one we're worried about,' the Sister said. 'His Apgar score is low, and he had asphyxia. His brother and his sister are doing fine. They're small, but they're fighters.'

Joanna went back to the babies' mother. She was drowsy, but awake enough to try to smile.

'Dr O'Connor has just been in,' she said. 'He came while my husband was here. And we know we have two boys and a girl. But he says the smallest one isn't doing as well as the other two. I want to see him, Sister, I want to see all my babies. And I don't want anything to happen to him—I want them all, I want them so much.'

Joanna took the young woman's hand in hers.

'Tomorrow morning, Pamela, we'll take you along to see your babies. And, yes, I know we're concerned about the tiniest one, but they're doing everything possible for him.' She looked up. 'Here's Night Sister to give you something for the pain and to help you to sleep. I'll be in first thing in the morning.'

She went back to the duty room slowly, her heart heavy as she collected her shoulder-bag and went along the corridor and down the stairs.

We do lose babies, she reminded herself, in spite of doing all we can to save them. But this little one means so much to his parents. I can't bear the thought of them losing him.

It was dark as she walked down the hill, and she was glad because she knew there were tears running down her cheeks.

'Joanna?'

He was there beside her, Jake, looking down at her.

'I saw you go,' he said. 'I came after you.'

He took both her hands in his.

'I thought nurses didn't get emotionally involved with their patients,' he said, very gently. He took out a large white handkerchief and dried her tear-wet cheeks awkwardly.

'I don't usually,' Joanna replied, her voice unsteady, 'but somehow I have this time. I know it isn't very professional.'

In the light of a streetlamp, his eyes were very dark as he looked down at her.

'Neither is this,' he said.

He took her face in both his hands and kissed her, his lips gentle and warm on hers.

'Can we talk, Joanna?' he asked her.

'If you want to,' she said uncertainly.

He smiled, a slow, warm smile.

'Oh, yes,' he said, and he spoke with complete certainty. 'Oh, yes, I want to. But not here.'

He took her hand, and she went with him, unresisting, back up the hill to his car. She felt as if she were in a dream, but a dream she didn't want to wake up from.

'We'll go over to the sea,' he said, and he drove across the city towards the sea. And there, with the sound of the waves breaking on the sand close to them, and the smell of the sea around them as he opened the windows, he turned to her.

'I don't know what to say now that I've got you here,' he said disarmingly. 'I've been a stubborn fool, Joanna. And too hurt and proud to admit it.'

'But you were right,' Joanna told him. 'You were right. I did judge you too quickly, I didn't give you a fair chance, I was much too—'

He stopped her with one finger on her lips.

'Are we going to waste any more time, telling each other how foolish we were?' he asked her. 'Or are going to get on with our lives?'

'I think we should...get on with our lives,' Joanna replied, not quite steadily because this man was so close to her and her heart was thudding unevenly.

'A very good idea, girl dear,' he murmured, just before his lips found hers.

It was a slow, warm kiss, gentle at first, and then not at all gentle, as they clung to each other, all the barriers gone, neither of them holding anything back.

At last, when they drew apart, he said, his lips against her hair, 'Well, now, that isn't at all bad for a start. What do you think, Joanna?'

'I think you're right,' Joanna agreed.

In the enclosed darkness of the car, she knew he was looking down at her.

'Perhaps I'd better take you home,' he said.

'I'm very happy right here,' Joanna assured him. 'But...'

'But what?' he asked, anxiety in his voice.

She sat up.

'But I'm very hungry,' she told him.

He gave a shout of laughter.

'Now that you mention it, I'm very hungry, too. We'll go and get something to eat, and then...'

'And then what?' Joanna asked him, demurely.

'And then we'll see,' he told her, laughing. 'Come along, girl dear.'

He took her hand in his.

'What I want,' Jake said later, much later, 'is for us to get married tomorrow. I guess that's a bit soon?'

'Married?' Joanna replied, drowsy and content, her head against his chest. 'I don't remember you asking me to marry you.'

'Are you sure I didn't say that somewhere along the line? I didn't? Well, I'm not going to get down on one knee, but here goes.' He raised himself on one elbow, and looked down at her, and the warm tenderness in the dark blue eyes brought a catch to her throat. 'Joanna, my love, my own darling girl, will you marry me?'

She knew that her answer was in her eyes, in her face, but she said it all the same.

'Oh, Jake, yes. Yes, I'll marry you.'

Even later, Jake said, 'Would you like us to do this in a traditional way, Joanna? Shall I court you, will we go out on dates and do the thing properly? Why are you laughing?' he demanded.

'Because you make it sound as if we've been doing things rather improperly,' she told him.

'Hmm—well, now, maybe you have a point. Seriously,

though, will we do it that way for a little while, then get engaged and then get married?' he asked her.

Joanna thought about that.

'It might be rather nice,' she said. 'After all, it's going to be my only chance at this courtship business. I may as well make the most of it.'

It was a wonderful time, a special time, she thought afterwards, for Jake did just what he had said. He courted her. He brought her flowers, and he took her to the theatre, to dinner, to parties where people could see that they were a couple.

And the rest of it, that was wonderful, too, because they had been so busy fighting each other, fighting the way they felt, that there hadn't been time for talking, time for just being together.

So they walked on the beach in the early morning, hand in hand, and Jake told her about his childhood in Ireland, and she told him about growing up in the cottage, about the close little family unit they had been, her mother and her father and her.

They took the cable-car to the top of Table Mountain, and stood high up, the wind blowing Joanna's hair, both of them breathless with the wind and with the beauty of the panorama spread beneath them. Then they sat in the little restaurant, and over tea and scones Jake told her about his mother and his father, retired now in a small village near Dublin.

'And my mother just about given up hope of a grandchild to hold on her knee, me being an only child,' he said mournfully. 'She'll be crying with joy when I phone to tell her we're getting married. You'll have to understand, of course, that from the day we get married she'll be waiting for the next news.'

That thought must have been in Joanna's mind for the

next day, when Jake had been called to do a difficult delivery, she looked at him holding the newborn baby and she thought of these same hands, strong and sure and confident, holding a child of his own, a child who was his and hers.

For a moment his eyes met hers, and she could see that he knew just what she was thinking. He smiled, and she smiled back.

In the duty room, as he was finishing his coffee, he said to her, 'Is it today Pamela Sutton is coming to take the baby home? You'll let me know when she comes, will you? I want to see that little fellow in his mother's arms, and going home to join his brother and his sister.'

In spite of all the odds, the smallest of the triplets had turned out to be a fighter, too, and although he'd had to stay at the hospital when the other two had been ready to go home he had made such good progress that now he was also ready to go home.

'How are they doing, the other two?' Joanna asked, when Pamela and her husband arrived later.

'They have us running around in circles,' Pamela told her. 'They work in shifts—one awake, one asleep, one hungry, the other needing a nappy change. What it will be like when Ricky here joins the team, I shudder to think.'

But she smiled up at her husband, and there was so much love in the way they looked at each other, the way she held her tiny baby, the way the father touched his small son gently, that Joanna's eyes blurred.

'I guess you won't be back to the infertility clinic, then,' Jake said, coming to say goodbye to them.

'I think we'll call it a day,' the young mother said, with heartfelt conviction.

'And a night, too,' her husband added. 'This lot haven't

learned the difference yet! Come on, Pam, we'd better get back—the two grannies are on duty, one baby each. We need a third one, don't we?'

Jake and Joanna watched them go along the corridor and turn to wave as they went into the lift.

'Happy ending,' Jake said with satisfaction. 'Or rather happy beginning. When are you off tonight? Should we go to a film? Oh, I'm on call. I'll have to be closer.'

'Come and have something to eat at the house,' Joanna suggested. She smiled. 'Now that you're officially accepted as my fiancé by my housemates.'

Which he was. Rose, Dorothy and David had got over their initial surprise and were obviously both intrigued and delighted.

And tactful.

When Jake arrived that evening, Dorothy had just told David that they were going out.

'I thought we were staying in and saving,' David said, surprised.

'We're not going out to spend a fortune,' his fiancée told him airily. 'Just—just out.' She frowned at him fiercely until he got the message. 'And, of course, Rose is on night duty,' she reminded Joanna as they went out.

As if I needed to be reminded, Joanna thought, smiling, as she went back to the kitchen to stir the bolognaise sauce and put on the pasta. All we need is for Jake not to be called.

But that had been too much to hope for, and a little while later she stood at the door with him.

'At least you had time to eat,' she pointed out.

He took her in his arms and kissed her. A long slow kiss, a kiss that ended with reluctance.

'The heck with this,' he said, not quite steadily. 'Let's get married, then at least I can come home to you.'

* * *

'A quiet wedding,' Dorothy repeated, clearly disappointed. 'How quiet?'

And a few days later, at Morgenster... 'A quiet wedding?' Alice said. 'How quiet?'

Joanna looked at Jake. And Alice looked at both of them.

'We could have a lovely quiet little wedding here,' she said eagerly. 'There's that little church in Stellenbosch, and we could have the reception here—the vines are so lovely in these early autumn days, just beginning to turn.'

She reached for her crutches, and walked across to Joanna, still a little stiff, a little awkward. But walking. Resting her crutches on the arm of the chair, she took both Joanna's hands.

'We're the closest to family you have here, the two of you,' she pointed out. 'I do accept that you want a quiet wedding, and it will be, but a really nice quiet wedding?'

Philip, who had come in just in time to hear that, shook his head.

'You might as well give in,' he told them. 'There's no holding Alice now that she can walk.' He smiled at his wife, and then he looked directly at Jake. 'Alice is right, though, Jake,' he said, a little awkwardly. 'We are the closest to family for both of you. More than that, for you and me. We are family, and I hope you'll let us do this.'

Jake looked at Joanna, and raised his eyebrows. Without needing to think about it, she nodded.

After that, things took off.

Alice had a dressmaker in Stellenbosch, and all Joanna had to do was to tell her the sort of dress she wanted.

'And she's going to make mine, too,' Cathy told them a few days later. 'For me to be your flower-girl.'

Cathy would be the only attendant, in spite of her suggestion that they could put a big bow round Simba's neck and he would walk beside her. And Jake and Joanna had managed to stand firm on the number of people invited so it really would be a quiet wedding, they kept assuring each other.

It had been raining overnight, but the sun was trying to break through the clouds on the morning of the wedding, and there was the first hint of autumn in the air. Jake had brought Joanna to the homestead the night before, and then, with reluctance, driven back to Cape Town to spend the night in the cottage they had bought in Camps Bay.

With Alice helping her, Joanna put on the slim sheath dress of cream raw silk and the big hat she had chosen instead of a veil.

'You look beautiful, Joanna,' Alice said softly.

I believe I do, Joanna thought, surprised and glad because she wanted to look beautiful today for Jake.

Cathy came in, having been dressed by Anna, her small face flushed with excitement.

'I look so pretty, don't I?' she said complacently, pirouetting round in her wide-skirted cream dress, with the pink rosebuds she had insisted on. And when her mother and Joanna had agreed, she said generously, 'You look pretty, too, both of you.'

Time, which had been passing slowly, suddenly seemed to gather momentum, and in no time, it seemed to Joanna, she and David were walking down the aisle together towards Jake, waiting for them with Philip beside him. David looked serious under the weight of his responsibilities, Joanna thought with affection. Thinking of his own wedding, in a few months, she was sure.

Jake watched her as she came towards him, and when she reached him he held out one hand to her. She put her hand into his, and she could see the wonder of the day reflected in his eyes. The service was short and simple, and soon they had exchanged rings and Jake was told he could kiss the bride. Soon after that, they were walking back down the aisle together to the triumphal wedding march.

Outside, they were showered with rose petals, handed to the guests by Cathy.

'Turn this way and smile, Joanna,' David called, changing from giver-away of the bride to photographer. Joanna watched him as he took other photos, photos that she knew would bring back the joy of this day.

Philip, helping Alice to balance her crutches, smiling down at her. Cathy, still scattering rose petals. Dorothy, giving David a quick kiss before he took her picture. Sister Kenton, looking as proud as if she had arranged the whole thing. Rose, talking to Anna, resplendent in a brightly flowered dress. Two of the doctors Jake worked with, with their wives.

A quiet wedding—just what we wanted, Joanna thought with satisfaction. The people we know, the people who have come to mean so much to us.

'Cathy wants her picture taken with the bride,' Jake said, beside her.

He held out his hand, and she put hers into it.

'Look,' he said, 'a rainbow.'

In the distant hills, where the clouds still lingered, there was a magnificent arc in the sky.

A promise, Joanna was sure, for all the years to come, for Jake and her.

The latest triumph from
international bestselling author
Debbie Macomber
MILLS & BOON®
brings you
PROMISE
Share the lives—and loves—of the
people in Promise, Texas.
A town with an interesting past
and an exciting future.
Available from 21st July
0008/114/MB5a